THE SATAN PIT

THE SATAN PIT

Based on the BBC television episodes
The Impossible Planet and *The Satan Pit*

MATT JONES

BBC Books, an imprint of Ebury Publishing

UK | USA | Canada | Ireland | Australia
India | New Zealand | South Africa

BBC Books is part of the Penguin Random House group of companies
whose addresses can be found at global.penguinrandomhouse.com

Penguin Random House UK
One Embassy Gardens, 8 Viaduct Gardens, London SW11 7BW

penguin.co.uk
global.penguinrandomhouse.com

First published by BBC Books in 2026

1

Novelisation and original script copyright © Matt Jones 2026
The moral right of the author has been asserted.

No part of this book may be used or reproduced in any manner for the
purpose of training artificial intelligence technologies or systems. In accordance
with Article 4(3) of the DSM Directive 2019/790, Penguin Random House
expressly reserves this work from the text and data mining exception.

Doctor Who is produced in Wales by Bad Wolf with BBC Studio Productions
Based on the BBC television adventures *The Impossible Planet*
and *The Satan Pit* by Matt Jones

Executive Producers: Russell T Davies, Julie Gardner,
Jane Tranter, Joel Collins & Phil Collinson

Typeset in 11.6/15pt Adobe Caslon Pro by Six Red Marbles UK, Thetford, Norfolk

Printed and bound in Great Britain by Clays Ltd, Elcograf S.p.A.

The authorised representative in the EEA is Penguin Random House Ireland,
Morrison Chambers, 32 Nassau Street, Dublin D02 YH68

A CIP catalogue record for this book is available from the British Library

ISBN 9781785949968

Publishing Director: Albert De Petrillo
Project Editor: Steve Cole
Cover Design: Two Associates
Cover Illustration: Dan Liles

Penguin Random House is committed to a sustainable future
for our business, our readers and our planet. This book is made
from Forest Stewardship Council® certified paper.

For Russell T Davies
Without whom . . .

Ida

Of course, what you really want to know about is the Doctor. Who he was. Where he came from. *What* he was. I'm afraid I don't have the answers to any of those questions. I only knew him for twelve hours, perhaps a little less.

I *can* tell you that, in that time, he completely and profoundly changed my life. Without him, I'd be dead. That much is certain. But because of what he did – what he had to do – I am sitting in an interrogation room about to be charged with causing the deaths of a dozen people and the destruction of an eighty-million-credit Sanctuary Base.

You might think I'd hold that against him. But then you've never met the Doctor.

He wasn't human, although he looked like one of us. He was handsome, not classically so, but he had an energy, a dynamism that I have never encountered before. Words tumbled out of him as if struggling to keep up with the thoughts sparking in his mind. I trusted him within moments of meeting him; within hours I depended on him for my life.

You're sceptical. Not only that he was as remarkable as I've described, but that he existed at all. Certainly, it makes it easier for you if he didn't. If Zack, Danny and I have invented him and his friend, Rose, then you can lay the blame for all those awful deaths at our feet. The cynic in me suspects you'd prefer it that way. Blame us, convict us, let the problem go away. Because, if what the Doctor said is true, then you'd have to accept that he looked the Devil in the eye and walked away to tell the tale. And that changes everything. Everything we know about the universe and our place in it. It means that our comforting reliance on reason and rationality is misplaced. That there are bigger questions to be asked, beyond science, beyond nature, beyond everything we know.

Even now, weeks after we returned, I can't begin to get my head around what happened to us, what we found on that impossible planet. And yet, if I'm going to have a chance at seeing daylight again, I must convince you that what I say is true. If I want to avoid spending the rest of my life in a penal colony, at least.

The interrogation room is twelve feet by seven. I know; I've paced it out three times. It's functional, but clean – a faint smell of industrial disinfectant suggests that things may take place in this room that require serious mopping up afterwards. There's a metal table, simple metal chairs that are screwed to the ground, and a small steel ring on my side of the table, where I imagine handcuffs can be fixed. I should be grateful for small mercies that my interrogators have not seen fit to cuff me to it.

Not yet at least.

Of the two of you, I prefer the cop. Kitzinger, right? Detective, Sandra. You do the talking. Your cropped hair – do you trim it yourself? – and crumpled, ancient overcoat suggest that you don't take bribes. Or if you do, you don't spend it on clothes. Your face is weatherbeaten, creased and reddened by stellar radiation. Like me, you've spent your life off world. You look like a woman I might be friends with.

I don't trust your colleague. She stays by the door and says little, but makes endless notes on her phone. With her fitted grey suit, stiletto heels and styled auburn hair, she reeks of Sanctuary Corps. Whilst you are focused on the deaths of the crew, she's more focused on the destruction of her eighty-million-credit deep space facility. Of the two of you, I'm more scared of her. At least you might give me a fair hearing.

You come back after leaving me alone for another chunk of time, which might be an hour or might be four, there's no clock on the wall. You settle down opposite me, take a sip from a thick, black coffee you have brought for yourself, before relighting the stub of your cigar, in defiance of the No Smoking sign on the interrogation room wall.

'I've spoken to your fellow crew members,' you inform me, through your smoker's cough. 'They confirm that two travellers arrived at Sanctuary Base 6, twelve hours before it was destroyed.'

'They *say* the travellers arrived,' the company suit interjects. 'I'm not taking their word for it.'

It's the first time I've heard your colleague speak. She sounds rich, educated. A senior exec. Sanctuary clearly mean business. She's here to ensure a conviction of malpractice, incompetence or sabotage in order to recoup the cost of the base from their insurers. Because they sure as hell aren't going to get eighty million out of me, Danny or Zack.

You shoot her a look. 'This is a police investigation. You're here as an observer. Don't make me remind you of that again.'

The suit raises her hands in mock deference. She's after my blood.

You ask me to start from the beginning. But where is that? I could tell you about my life before the expedition. Why I made the certifiable decision to travel somewhere balanced impossibly within the gravitational pull of a black hole. But, like I said, you don't want to know about that.

You want to know about the Doctor.

Jefferson met them first. I was battening down the hatches, preparing for another quake. The tremors were coming so frequently now that I feared that they might shake the base apart. My fears were not without foundation. We had assembled the base when we arrived, fastening the skeletal architecture together with giant bolts and screws. Despite Sanctuary's assurances, I wasn't convinced the giant temporary steel structure could withstand an earthquake's destructive power. Even when the planet beneath us was still, the metal walkways clattered under foot and the walls creaked and groaned. Few of us slept easy in our beds.

Jefferson came over the comms to tell us about the visitors. Which, like most things that involved the Doctor, was impossible. At first, I thought Jefferson was being metaphorical. The crew sometimes talked about the planetary debris that swirled above us before being crushed out of existence as visitors. I was so wrapped up in my duties that I wasn't prepared for strangers walking into the command centre. But then I don't know how I could have prepared myself. We were living on a dead planet, orbiting a black hole. The last thing you would expect is guests. But there they were, grinning like a couple of tourists on a guided tour.

'People!' Scooti exclaimed next to me. 'Look at that! Real people.'

'That's us! Hooray!' the Doctor replied. His voice was bright and welcoming. Almost familiar. Which was ridiculous. I was certain I had never seen him before in my life. And he wasn't the sort of person you'd easily forget.

'Definitely real,' added the young woman I would shortly come to know as Rose Tyler.

As they introduced themselves, Scooti was not the only one freaking out. Danny checked the life support readings on the screen in front of him.

'No way, come on, the oxygen readings must be offline. We're hallucinating, they can't be ...' He actually went up to them open mouthed and gently squeezed the Doctor's arm. 'No, they're real, they're really real, you can touch them!'

The Doctor looked a little bemused, but not hostile, as it if wasn't the first time that his mere presence had engendered disbelief. He stuffed his hands in the pockets of his trousers, which matched his jacket, suggesting some kind of uniform, except his grin and relaxed attitude left you with an impression of a life lived without discipline.

Zack was the only one of us who hadn't lost the plot in the face of the impossible couple. He kept his focus on the seismograph in front of him, his broad shoulders hunched as he leant over the machine, the light from the screen illuminating his face. 'Come on, we're in the middle of an alert. Danny, strap up, the quake's coming in. Seconds to impact!'

He told the Doctor and Rose to hang on to something, as the first tremor rattled the equipment on the console.

'That wasn't so bad,' the Doctor shrugged, relaxing his grip on the safety rail, which was exactly when the quake hit, almost knocking him off his feet.

'Deflecting to Storage Bays 5 to 8,' Zack shouted, using the base's fields to deflect the kinetic energy to an uninhabited area of the habitat. But the force of the quake in the command centre still exceeded the tolerance of some of the instruments and they burst into flames. Jefferson was on them in a moment, moving purposefully, ripping an extinguisher from its bracket and dousing the small fires with foam. The command centre was suddenly full of a dry chemical tang that tasted worse than the smoke. He squeezed my arm and asked if I was okay. Since the death of the Captain, Jefferson was the oldest member of the crew and, whilst he wasn't in charge and never tried to be, he had assumed a quiet paternal role, which I sometimes found patronising, but never in moments of crisis.

Zack sent Toby to check on the rocket-link, which he didn't like, claiming it wasn't his department. Like any of us were only doing the work on our job descriptions any more. Eight months in space and people's irritating mannerisms could work your last nerve. Toby stormed out of the command centre, which is always easier said than done, as you have to wait for the computer to unlock the pressure seals on the door, and then announce that it has. We'd all been there; had a meltdown and flounced away, only to face a ten-second pause where we endured the humiliation of staring at a closed door. The difference between Toby and the rest of us was we'd all realise we were making fools of ourselves and slope back with an embarrassed grin.

In a moment of pathetic fallacy, the storm rattled the roof of the hub as he waited for the door to open, and then he stomped away down the corridor. Scooti rolled her eyes. I wasn't the only one who found Toby infuriating.

'Never mind the earthquake, that's a hell of a storm,' Rose said, looking up at the ceiling, which creaked menacingly. 'What is it, a hurricane?'

Scooti turned to look at Rose, bemused. 'You need an atmosphere to have a hurricane. There's no air out there. Complete vacuum.'

I'd had the same thought as Scooti. How was it possible that they didn't know what was outside?

'Then what's shaking the roof?'

'You're not kidding? You've got no idea?' I said, joining them. I introduced the crew and then myself. After which, I pulled the control that operated the observation window, and let them see exactly where we had been calling home for the last eight months. The two curved panels of the observatory slid smoothly open, revealing, in all its glory, the thing that had brought us here. It filled the command centre with a rich, orange glow, which had become the colour of my nightmares.

'Brace yourselves,' Zack said. 'The sight of it drives some people mad.'

'That's ... that's a black hole,' Rose stammered.

The Doctor turned to face me, his eyes wide. 'But that's impossible ...'

It was the first time I had seen him lose his composure. He was the cleverest man I'd ever met. Will ever meet, I'm sure. His mind was racing so quickly, I could almost feel the thoughts forming in his head.

'I did warn you,' Zack added unhelpfully.

'We're standing underneath a black hole ...' the Doctor stammered.

I smiled. 'In orbit.'

'We can't be.'

'We're in orbit.'

'But we can't be,' the Doctor repeated, as if repeating it would stop it be being true.

'This lump of rock is suspended in perpetual geostationary orbit around the Black Hole. Without falling in. Discuss,' I added, with, I confess, a self-satisfied smirk.

Rose was affected by the Doctor's bewilderment. She looked between us, anxiously. 'And ... that's bad, yeah?' I could see she wasn't used to the Doctor being out of his depth.

'Bad doesn't cover it,' the Doctor started. 'A black hole's a dead star, it collapses in on itself, in and in and in, until the matter's so dense and tight, it starts to pull everything else in too. Nothing in the universe can escape it. Light, gravity, time, everything gets pulled inside. And crushed.'

As explanations went, it was both concise and accurate.

'So ... there can't be an orbit?' Rose was trying to get her head around the impossible. 'We should be pulled right in?'

The Doctor continued to stare up into the night. 'We should be dead.'

I followed his gaze. It was looking particularly spectacular that night. The larger planets of the Coral System had broken up a few million years ago and the debris of gas and dust was feeding the orange halo of the accretion disk. Within that surprisingly bright halo was a circle of darkness, so total, so complete, that it denied the existence of everything that came within its reach. Zack was right: no one should look at it for too long. Not if they wanted to stay sane.

'And yet, here we are. Beyond the laws of physics. Welcome on board.'

'But if there's no atmosphere out there,' Rose asked, pointing to the planetary debris. 'What are those clouds?'

I told her about the different clouds that form in space. Clouds of gas and dust. Stars breaking up. Whole solar systems being ripped apart, before falling into that thing.

'So ... bit worse than a storm, then.'

'Just a bit.'

I confess I wrote Rose off when I first met her. She had no scientific background and lacked the Doctor's compelling brilliance. I could not have been more wrong. She was just as remarkable as him, perhaps more so, because she matched him for courage and decency, despite lacking his extraordinary mind. Her clothes were as unusual as his. Her hair had been lightened and she had drawn what looked like charcoal lines around her eyes, perhaps to accentuate them. Her styling was primitive, and if it was designed to make her look more attractive to potential mates, then it was lacking in any subtlety.

However, it would be Rose's courage and decency that would save us all. I may have dismissed her as merely the Doctor's assistant or lover, but when I looked across the room and saw Danny staring at her, I realised that she had someone's full attention.

Danny

Okay! I admit it – I lied. I shouldn't have said that Zack told me to monitor the new arrivals. He didn't. You got me! I didn't realise that you were going to ask the others to corroborate every single detail of my statement! To tell you the truth, I was embarrassed, so I told a white lie. A little fib. Nothing more than that. Rose was the first woman to arrive on the base since we left mission control and ... I was intrigued by her. More than that, I fancied her! There, I said it. Eight months is a long time to be involuntarily single. Particularly when you've been friend-zoned by every woman less than five light years away.

But that doesn't mean that I misled you about anything else. Every word I've told you is true.

Except for that bit.

I signed up for this mission to meet a girl like Rose. My life was a boring routine: work, gym, dinner, repeat. Something had to give. I read about the mission and thought, this is what I've been waiting for. The chance to make something of my life. And to meet some new people. Female people. But it was the same story on the hell planet as it was back home. *I think of you as a friend.* And so my life on Sanctuary Base 6 became exactly the same as it had been before – work, gym, dinner. Until one day, Rose Tyler walked into the command centre and I thought, this is it, this must be destiny, because it was literally impossible for her to be here.

She had to be here for me.

My initial attempt to speak to her failed. I'd planned to go over and squeeze her arm to 'see if I'm hallucinating, ha ha' (I read in a dating guide that you can make a good impression with a gentle, unthreatening touch) but I mistimed it and ended up squeezing the Doctor's arm instead. Fortunately, he didn't take offence, but then they were dragged away by Ida and the other grown-ups at the command console. So, feeling like a fifth wheel, I had no choice but to slip back to the junior station, where Scooti shot me a look to say – *could you be more obvious?* I was resigned to sneaking glances over at Rose, whilst eavesdropping on the conversation around the console. Zack was showing them a hologram I'd seen a hundred times.

'That's the Black Hole, officially designated K 37 Gem 5,' he pointed out.

Ida filled in the new arrivals with the background to the project. 'In the scriptures of the Veltino, this planet's called Krop Tor – the bitter pill. The Black Hole's supposed to be a mighty demon who was tricked into devouring the planet only to spit it out, because it was poison.'

'The bitter pill,' Rose grinned. 'I like that.'

She had an amazing smile. Scooti must have seen me staring, because she coughed pointedly and indicated the screen full of tasks waiting for my attention.

The Doctor frowned as he took in the hologram of the Black Hole. 'We're so far out. Lost in the drifts of the universe. How did you even get here?'

Zack manipulated the image. 'We flew in, d'you see?'

The hologram zoomed in on the planet, which filled the space above the console, and showed the twister-like funnel of the gravity field, spiralling out from the surface. Zack explained that it was being generated somewhere in the depths of the planet.

Rose was intrigued. 'You flew down that thing?' she said, flashing that smile again. 'Like a rollercoaster.'

I had no idea what a rollercoaster was, but, from the astonishment on her face, I'd definitely like to find out.

'By rights, the ship should've been torn apart,' Zack explained. 'We lost the Captain, that's what put me in charge.'

'And you're doing a good job,' Ida reassured him.

'Yeah well, needs must.'

There was a pause in the conversation, so I took my chance and butted in: 'But if that gravity funnel closes, there's no way out.'

Rose glanced in my direction.

'Oh, we have fun speculating about that!' Scooti joined in.

'Yeah, that's the word, fun,' I added lightly, but Rose had already returned her attention to the hologram of the planet. Damn!

'That field would take phenomenal amounts of power,' the Doctor said. 'Not just big, but off the scale.' He grabbed a calculator off the console. 'Can I?'

Without waiting for permission, he punched numbers so quickly that it was hard to believe he was being serious.

An Ood approached Rose with a cup of water. It activated its translator, illuminating its mouth of fleshy fronds. 'Your refreshment,' it said, in its artificially generated voice.

'Oh, yeah, thanks,' Rose said, taking the cup. Then she seemed to remember her manners. 'Thank you! I'm sorry, what was your name?'

The Ood cocked its bald, wrinkled head. 'We have no titles,' it replied, before walking away.

For a moment, Rose was alone. I wasn't going to miss this opportunity and headed over. She was staring at the Ood's retreating figure, when I reached her side.

'They're called the Ood.'

'The Ood?'

'The Ood.'

'Well, that's ... Ood.'

It was an old joke. The oldest. But she made it feel fresh. She'd clearly never heard of them before, which didn't make any kind of sense. Where the hell had she grown up?

'They work the mineshaft, all the drilling and stuff, supervision and maintenance.' I realised I was babbling. 'They're born for it. Basic slave race.'

She frowned. 'You've got slaves?'

'Oh, don't you start!' Scooti chimed in, joining us. Not that anyone had invited her. 'She's like that lot, Friends of the Ood.'

Rose turned on her. 'Well, maybe I am, yeah? Since when did humans need slaves?'

'It's their choice,' I said, defensively. 'The Ood offer themselves, they want to serve. If you don't give them orders, they just pine away and die.'

'Seriously?' Rose sounded incredulous. She headed over to speak to another Ood that was clearing away some drinks. 'You like being ordered about?'

I wasn't sure how the conversation had gotten away from me. How was it possible that she was more interested in talking to a squidmouth than me? The woman was a complete mystery. One that I intended to solve. I was going to make her fall for me, if it was the last thing I did. And that's why I decided to use the station cameras to learn as much about her as I could.

That's the truth. The whole truth. Nothing but. You can intimidate me all you want, blow cigar smoke in my face. But I didn't kill anyone. They were my friends. Jefferson, Scooti and the others. I didn't destroy your base. I've told you what I did a hundred times and you're never going to believe me. Just like you're not going to believe me about that impossible couple who saved us all.

Zack

The Doctor finished his calculations and brandished the calculator with a flourish. 'There we go! D'you see? To generate that gravity field, and the funnel, you need a power source with an inverted self-extrapolating reflex of six to the power of six, every six seconds.'

'That's all the sixes,' his companion said, joining us.

'And, it's impossible,' the Doctor added, removing his glasses and rubbing the bridge of his nose.

I stared at him for a long moment, unsure whether to take him seriously. Oh, the calculation was correct. I had good reason to know that it was. 'It took me two years to work that out,' I told the Doctor, struggling to keep the incredulity out of my voice. Had he really reached the same result in less than a minute?

'I'm very good,' the Doctor said with a grin.

I understand how you don't believe someone like the Doctor could exist. I can hardly believe it myself – and I met him! The truth was, he was more than any of us could have imagined. He reminded me of the Captain. She was charismatic, just like the Doctor, and filled a room with energy and humour just as he did. Half of us signed up for this mission because of her. She made the prospect of travelling halfway across the galaxy to live beneath a black hole seem like a good idea. I'd worked for her off and on for years – her trusted Number Two. People were always vying for her attention, which she loved of course. The Court of Captain O'Donnell. Being by her side made you feel special. A bit of her status rubbing off on you.

Her personality too. I ended up picking up some of her mannerisms, her ways of speaking. She had these little catchphrases, just like the Doctor. She was a lot like him in many ways. And I knew in my heart of hearts that I was no match for her leadership. Nor his, come to think of it.

The Doctor listened carefully as Ida described the drilling operation. Ten miles vertically down to find the power source that kept the gravity funnel in operation. It was giving off readings of over ninety Statts on the Blazen Scale. That in itself was reason enough to cross the galaxy. Or as Ida more poetically put it:

'It could revolutionise modern science. Fuel the Empire.'

'Or start a war,' the Doctor said, quietly. His eyes scanned our faces, as if he were trying to read our true motives in our minds.

'It's buried beneath us. In the darkness. Waiting.'

I turned at the sound of Toby's voice; he had returned from checking on the supply rocket. The overhead light shadowed his eyes.

The young woman, Rose Tyler, raised an eyebrow. 'What's your job? Chief dramatist?'

The Doctor smirked. Toby didn't. He'd been the Captain's appointment. I'd never understood what she'd seen in him. As far as I could see, Toby Zed was a humourless jobsworth. The Captain thought he had an affinity for his subject. A passion for the work.

Turns out she was right. But in ways none of us could ever have imagined.

'Whatever it is, down there,' Toby continued, ignoring Rose's jibe, 'it's not a natural phenomenon. This planet once supported life, aeons ago, before the human race had even learnt to walk.'

The Doctor asked him about the writing that had been unearthed by the drilling. Toby admitted he'd been unable to translate it.

'Neither can I,' the Doctor murmured, half to himself. 'And that's saying something.'

'There was some form of civilisation,' Toby continued. 'They buried something. And now it's reaching out. Calling us in.'

The Doctor watched him for a long moment, his forehead cut into a frown. 'And you came,' he murmured, not taking his eyes off Toby.

'How could we not?' Ida chipped in brightly.

The Doctor broke out of his reverie. 'So when it comes right down to it, why did you come here? Why did you do that? Why? I'll tell you why! Because it was there! Brilliant! 'Scuse me, Zack, wasn't it?'

'That's me,' I said, unsure what was coming.

The Doctor fixed me in his gaze, a grin hovering around his mouth. 'Just stand there, cos I'm going to hug you, is that all right?'

The question was ridiculous, the delivery so theatrical, that all I could do was shrug. 'Um. Suppose so,' I managed.

'Here we go. Coming in.'

He slipped his arms around me and pulled me into a surprisingly tight hug. I ended up with my face in his neck, which impossibly smelt of the outdoors: fresh air and wet grass. I was hit by a wave of nostalgia for home. All I'd known for the last eight months was recycled air and water, which smelt and tasted of chemical purifiers.

'Human beings,' the Doctor said, giving my shoulders a squeeze. 'You are amazing. Thank you.'

'Not at all,' I said, still reeling from the smell of, if not home, then somewhere other than this godforsaken world.

The Doctor stuffed his hands in his suit pockets. 'But apart from that, you're completely mad! You should pack your bags, get back on that ship and fly for your lives!'

Ida wasn't having it. 'You're hardly one to talk. And how did you get here?'

It was only then that I realised that this question hadn't occurred to me. There was something about the Doctor's manner that had led me to simply accept his sudden presence amongst us. His explanation for their arrival – that his ship 'just sort of appears' – was pretty implausible.

Rose could see I didn't buy it. 'We can show you, we parked just down the corridor from – what was it called, Habitation Area 3 . . . ?

'D'you mean Storage 6?' I asked.

'It was a bit of a cupboard, yeah . . .' the Doctor said, having the same thought that I was. 'Storage 6?' he turned to Zack. 'But you said . . . You said Storage 5 to 8 . . .'

He bolted across the room and hammered on the control stud to open the door.

'*Opening Door 1,*' the computer intoned neutrally.

'Come on, c'mon!'

Rose was at his side in a second. 'What is it? What's wrong?'

But the Doctor was already spinning the door mechanism.

Ida and I exchanged glances. I could see that she was way ahead of the Doctor's friend. I indicated that I'd go with them.

The Doctor had run all the way to Habitation 3 when I caught up with them. He was trying to access the corridor to the storage section beyond.

'Oh these doors, c'mon!' he yelled.

I followed more slowly. I knew what was coming. From the panic in the Doctor's voice, I'm sure the Doctor did too. He just didn't want to face it. He opened the door to the Area 3 Walkway, sprinted along it and tried without success to get the computer to open the door to the storage unit.

'*Door 16 out of commission. This area is unsafe. Repeat, this area is unsafe.*'

'What's wrong?' Rose was saying. 'What is it? Doctor, the TARDIS is in there, what's happened?'

The Doctor gave up trying to open the door. As I arrived, he turned to Rose, to tell her what we had already worked out:

'The TARDIS has gone.'

She stared at him blankly, so he opened the viewing panel in the door. Over her shoulder, I could see the rocky surface of the planet, dust storms sweeping across the landscape and beyond that, the Black Hole dominating the sky.

'The earthquake. This section collapsed.'

'But ... it's got to be out there somewhere,' she stammered.

'Look down.'

Rose pressed her face right up against the glass and did as he told her to. I'd already seen what was out there on the monitors in the command centre. A deep, black crevasse. An endless pit, heading down into the dark.

The Doctor turned to me, desperation on his face. I knew what was coming.

'My ship must've fallen down, right into the heart of the planet. You've got robot drills, heading the same way ...'

'We can't divert the drilling,' I told him.

'But I need my ship! It's all I've got! Literally the only thing!'

'Doctor, we've only got the resources to dig one central shaft down to the power source, and that's it. No diversions, no distractions, no exceptions. Your machine is lost.'

He was about to argue when I cut him off. It was time for me to exert my command. I may not have felt like a leader – it certainly wasn't a role I would have chosen for myself – but it was the role that fate had carved out for me. 'All I can do is offer you a lift, if we ever get to leave this place. That's the end of it.'

Danny

We didn't use the cameras on the base very often. When we did, it was usually to look for faults and stress fractures caused by the tremors. If anyone caught me looking at security footage, they'd have questions, so I had to wait till I had a break before I could slip to my room and access the cameras without anyone looking over my shoulder.

When I watched their ship appear, I understood why they were so upset to have lost it. The shadows in the corner of the storage bay seemed to coalesce into the outline of their – I'm still not sure what to call it – capsule? Like most things on the base, the security monitors had seen better days. The footage they produced was grainy and the audio kept breaking up. The audio must've been on the blink now, because the ship's engines sounded like the death throes of an animal. One moment it wasn't there and then, in just a few seconds, it was.

I know what you're thinking: matter transmission is still theoretical. And I agree, it is. But if I was lying, why would I make up something so implausible? Why didn't I say they came in a Scout Ship or a Corsair that made planetfall and docked with our airlock? Because I'm telling you the truth, even when it's not to my advantage. The Doctor had access to technology years beyond our understanding. He had this little handheld tool that could do pretty much anything – repair electrical systems, make medical scans, open doors. It was insane that so much tech could be packed into something the size of a pen. His capsule was the same, totally beyond our comprehension.

As he stepped out of it, he patted it affectionately, as if it were alive.

'She's sort of queasy. Indigestion. Like she didn't want to land.'

Rose stepped out after him and took in the storage bay. 'If you think there's gonna be trouble, we could always get back inside and go somewhere else.'

The provocation hung in the air between them, and then they burst out laughing, as if the idea that they might do something so sensible was absurd. I wondered how they felt about their decision to stay now. I scrolled past their meeting with the Ood and then Jefferson and his team.

The live feed picked them up in Habitation 3, watching the Black Hole with Ida, who was pointing out the demise of a solar system.

'That used to be the Scarlet System. Home to the Pallushi. A mighty civilisation, spanning a billion years, disappearing forever. Their planets, suns, consumed. We have witnessed its passing.'

She went to close the roof, but the Doctor stopped her. 'Could you leave it open? Just for a bit? I won't go mad, I promise.'

'How would you know?' Zack observed dryly from the command console, before ordering the team to attend to tasks throughout the base. Rose was left alone with the Doctor, making me acutely aware that I was eavesdropping, but I couldn't help myself.

'I've seen films and things, they say black holes are like gateways to another universe.'

'Not that one,' the Doctor answered. 'It just ... eats.'

They stared up at the night for a long moment.

'Long way from home,' Rose said quietly.

The Doctor pointed through the observation window above them. 'Go that way. Turn right. Keep going for, oh 500 years, and then you'll reach the Earth.'

Rose pulled what I assumed to be a communicator out of her pocket. I didn't recognise the design. 'No signal. First time we've gone out of range. Mind you, even if I could ... what would I say to her?'

The Doctor didn't reply, just continued to stare up into the night.

Finally, Rose asked: 'Couldn't you build another TARDIS?'

Was that what their capsule was called?

'They were grown, not built. And with my home planet gone, we're kinda stuck.'

'Well,' Rose said, sounding like something was stuck in her throat. 'Could be worse. This lot said they'd give us a lift.'

I wished I knew her better so I could comfort her. Couldn't her friend see that she was upset?

The Doctor shrugged. 'And then what?'

'I dunno. Find a planet. Get a job. Earn some money. Live a life. Same as the rest of the universe.'

'I'd have to settle down. Get a house or something. A proper house. With doors and things. And carpets. Me! Living in a house!' He started to laugh. 'Now that is terrifying!'

I watched Rose join in, burying her distress or perhaps lifted out of it by his humour. He had a knack for doing that. 'You'd have to get a mortgage!'

'No!' The Doctor exclaimed, horrified.

'Oh yes!'

'I'm dying,' he laughed. 'That's it, I'm dying, it's all over.'

'What about me?' she asked. No trace of the sadness that had been in her voice a moment before. 'I'd have to get one too! Well, I dunno, could be the same one, we could both . . .' She paused, suddenly awkward. 'Or not. Whatever. I dunno. All sorts of . . .'

'Anyway!' the Doctor said brightly, changing the subject.

'We'll see,' Rose finished uncomfortably.

That same cold shame of rejection landed in my guts like a stone. She loved him. No, she was in love with him. He didn't know. Had no idea. The irony was not lost on me. Her staring at his uncomprehending face, just as I was watching hers on my screen.

They were still talking, more serious now.

'I promised Jackie I would always take you back home,' the Doctor said.

Rose said, with an acceptance I could see she didn't really feel, 'Everyone leaves home, in the end.'

'Not to end up stuck here.'

'Yeah, but . . .' Her voice trailed off for a moment. 'Stuck with you. That's not so bad.'

It was a declaration of sorts. Understated, but clear in its intent. This time he didn't miss it.

'Yeah?' he asked, looking right at her.

'Yeah,' she replied, meeting his gaze.

He loved her too.

Just my luck.

I was about to turn off the screen and head back to work, when a musical alert sounded. It was a simple two-note refrain, not from any device on the base. On screen, Rose put the communicator to her ear. She listened for a moment and then threw it to the ground as if it had stung her.

My attention was distracted by another camera feed. A thumbnail in the corner of my screen. It was Toby in his lab. He must have been lying on the floor, because the movement that snagged my attention was him suddenly sitting up. Only he did it at the exact moment that Rose violently threw her device.

'What did it say?' the Doctor's tinny voice came over the speaker.

'*He is awake.*'

I watched Toby stagger to his feet. He looked disorientated, as if he had just come to. At the time, I thought it was just a coincidence – Toby waking up, just as Rose received the same message, but something about Toby's behaviour troubled me. He was staring into space, and his face looked . . .

It's easy to say this with hindsight, but I swear I thought it at the time. It was an expression I hadn't seen on his face before. I'd seen him look pissed off. I'd seen him look superior. But I'd never seen him look like this.

He looked . . . cruel.

I sped back through the footage in the lab to try and find out what had caused Toby to collapse. I paused the recording when I found him sitting at his workstation, staring at the pieces of relics the drill had spat out, inscribed with the language of the civilisation that made all this. It took me a moment to realise what had made me stop there. Toby had stiffened in his chair, half turned. But when I played the moment in real time, there was nothing that could have snagged his attention – no one behind him or in the corridor outside the lab. He must've thought he heard something, because he called out a name.

My name.

'Dan?' he said, uncertainly. 'That's not Dan ...'

At the time I thought he was having some kind of breakdown. He was always a little bubble off normal. 'Who are you?' I heard him say, his voice trembling. 'If I could ...'

He gestured that he wanted to turn around, but then froze, looking terrified. He was definitely having a conversation with someone – or thought he was. Because whoever he thought he was talking to was only in his head. He became increasingly agitated, throwing down the archaeological relics he'd been holding and ripping off his latex gloves. He rubbed frantically at his hands as if they were stained and then ran to a mirror and tore violently at his face. It was as if he were trying to wipe something awful away. But whatever it was that was so terrifying was only showing itself to him.

I know what you're thinking. And Toby was always pretty unstable, I'll admit that. But this was something else. Something got inside him. I wish to God I'd realised that at the time, because if I had, more of my friends might have survived.

I was heading back to my shift, passing through Door 3. As I spun the wheel to open the door, the computer intoned, '*Open Door 3.*' Just as it always did. But when I went to close it behind me, instead of saying '*Close Door 3,*' it said:

'*He is awake.*'

I hesitated. 'What did you say?'

I wasn't mistaken, because it said it again, in its flat, emotionless voice.

'*He is awake.*'

I asked the computer to run an immediate diagnostic on the door, but it didn't respond, so I ran my own brand of diagnostic on it and gave it a good thump.

'*Close Door 3,*' it stated, apparently back to normal.

By the time I arrived back at the holding pen, I had forgotten all about the glitch with the door. Weird crap like that was always happening on the base. It wasn't just planetary debris that was being pulled into the Black Hole: radio emissions, dark matter, neutrinos and electromagnetic radiation were bent out of shape by it. Anything that crossed the event horizon was crunched into non-existence. We were used to hearing lost signals from forgotten civilisations suddenly come through our monitors. Out of context and out of time. We once heard a president declare nuclear war. Another time, we heard a performance of an entire play in a language that had been dead for centuries.

The Ood were quiet when I entered the holding pen. They were seated, heads bowed a little. Off duty. I climbed down into the pen, confronted not for the first time by their stale smell, like a well-maintained zoo. I ran through a basic inspection, but my heart wasn't in it. To be honest, I was feeling distracted. A few moments later, the cause of my distraction arrived with her friend.

'Only us!' Rose called out, as she and the Doctor appeared on the walkway above the pen.

'The mysterious couple!' I quipped, as I climbed up to join them. I was still hoping that Rose might correct my assumption, but being described as a couple didn't bother her in the least. I asked them how they were settling in, but the Doctor wasn't in the mood for small talk.

'Yeah, sorry, straight to business. The Ood, how do they communicate? I mean, with each other?'

'Oh, just empaths. There's a low-level telepathic field connecting them. Not that it does them much good. They're basically a herd race. Like cattle.'

The Doctor frowned. I could tell he didn't approve of me talking about them like that. 'This telepathic field, can it pick up messages?'

Rose interrupted: 'Cos I was having dinner, and one of the Ood, it said something... well, odd.'

'An odd Ood,' I smiled, but this time she didn't smile back. She was worried. I tried to be helpful, but when I asked her what the Ood had said, she quoted something that sounded like old religious nonsense.

'The Beast and all his armies shall rise from the Pit to make war against God.'

I told them about the stray transmissions, but it didn't reassure her.

'I got something else on my, um –' she glanced at the Doctor – 'communicator thing.'

I tried to look as if this was news to me. Did she know I'd been spying on her? Was that why they were here? I felt myself flush with shame. That would be so humiliating.

'It said,' she continued, '*He is awake.*'

I relaxed. All I could think about was – I was off the hook. 'I had a door say the same thing to me. Look, our systems are vulnerable to all kinds of signal distortion out here.'

'Whatever it was,' Rose insisted, 'it wasn't a stray transmission.'

'If there was something wrong, it would show – we monitor the Ood's telepathic field, it's the only way to look after them. They're so stupid, they don't even tell us when they're ill.'

The Doctor had moved over to the console that monitored the Ood's life signs. 'Monitor the field ... that's this thing?' He moved his hands swiftly over the controls, expertly bringing up the current status of the telepathic field.

'Yeah but, like I said, it's low-level telepathy, they only register Basic 5.'

The Doctor swung the monitor around to face me. The telepathic wave on the readout was agitated. The number it reported was spiralling upwards.

Basic 7 ... Basic 12 ... Basic 20 ... It showed no sign of slowing down.

'That's not Basic 5,' the Doctor said, stating the obvious. 'They've gone up to Basic 30.'

I looked at the screen. It should have been impossible, but there it was. Nothing in my training had prepared me to deal with it. 'But ... they can't.'

Rose tugged the Doctor's arm. 'Doctor, look, the Ood ...'

Down in the pen, the Ood were all staring up at us. They were silent, unmoving, and they were doing something I had never seen them do before. They were glaring at us. They were angry.

'What does Basic 30 mean?' Rose asked, next to me.

That level of psychokinetic energy was enough to have shattered the viewing ports. Basic 20 was enough to turn their brains to mush. 'It means they're shouting. Screaming. Inside their heads.'

The Doctor took out a piece of tech I didn't recognise. He waved it over the Ood, like a wand, and then checked a reading on it. 'Or something is shouting at them.'

'But . . . where's it coming from? What's it saying?'

'Presumably, *He is awake*,' the Doctor said grimly.

The Ood spoke for the first time, communicator globes illuminated in front of them. Five words in unison. Like a chant.

'And you will worship him.'

I'd never heard an Ood raise its voice before. They weren't meant to get upset or angry. They weren't meant to do anything other than what they were told.

The Doctor repeated himself – 'He is awake' – and the Ood chanted right back at us.

'And you will worship him.'

The Doctor grabbed the rail of the walkway, staring down, horrified. 'Worship who? Who's talking to you? Who is it?'

But the Ood wouldn't answer. They only stared up at us from the darkened pen, their eyes brighter than I'd ever seen them before. The silence was unnerving.

It didn't last long.

Zack

The Captain was the first person to die on the mission. One of the port shields blew as we entered the gravity funnel. Someone had to repair the damage or the ship was going to be torn apart before we'd make landfall. The only way to access the site of the damage was to put on a spacesuit and walk across the hull. The Captain was the only member of the crew with the skillset to make the repair. Of course, she loved the idea. It was that kind of crazed heroism she lived for. As she fixed the helmet over her orange survival suit, she grinned at me and said, 'Either way, it's a great story.'

I never saw her again. A glitch in the software in her suit demagnetised her boots for a quarter of a second and she was gone. When I stepped up to command, I vowed no one would die on my watch. To hell with whatever was buried down there in the planet, my first priority was to get everyone home alive.

My failure still haunts me every day.

I didn't pay much attention when Scooti reported a malfunctioning door over the comms. 'It's saying that someone's gone outside, onto the planet's surface. Zack? Zack?'

Living beneath an event horizon meant that the tech was always glitching. We were within a day of the drill reaching its target and we were running on fumes. Our last functioning drill head was in constant danger of overheating, and we'd long since run out of coolant. I thought a malfunctioning door could wait.

Turns out I was wrong.

Scooti's voice was so much background noise. The comms channels were always full of requests, questions and sometimes just chat. The interference meant that we couldn't trust text-based messaging. You could never be sure that the person you'd sent the message to had received it, or if the reply had come from them or was in response to a question you'd asked yesterday. There were complaints when I banned it, but glitches cost lives. We'd learnt that to our cost.

I was hunched over the console, using force fields to try and keep the drill vertical. They weren't designed for it, but I was running out of options. I was operating the fields by hand; it was beyond our computer's capabilities. I remember feeling irritated that Scooti's voice was still burbling in my ear.

'Computer, trace fault,' I heard her say.

'There is no fault,' the computer replied.

I was annoyed that she'd left the comms open. If I'd had a free hand, I would have told her to get off the channel.

'Tell me,' she said. 'Who went through that door?'

'He is awake.'

'What?'

'He is awake.'

'What's that supposed to mean?'

I cursed under my breath. She was arguing with bloody radio interference!

'He bathes in the black sun.'

I felt a chill despite myself. Sometimes we'd hear snippets of broadcasts and they'd seem to relate to our situation. It was ridiculous of course. Or so we thought.

Scooti started babbling then. She kept saying that there was no air. I didn't know what she meant, but the tone of her voice alarmed me. I risked letting the automatics control the drill for a moment and reached out to her on the channel. She didn't reply, at least not to me.

She was yelling. 'No! Stop it! You can't be . . .'

I'd never heard her sound so scared, or so young.

And then everything went to hell.

Alerts sounded across the base. Every sensor that was still working was telling me that the hull was experiencing stresses beyond its tolerance. A shudder ran through the length of the base and knocked me off my feet. I lay on my back for a moment, stunned. I felt the foundations shift beneath me with a low groan. It wasn't a quake or the Black Hole. We weren't being shaken up or pulled apart. We were being crushed in something's grip. Some enormous pressure was exerting itself on the entire base. It was impossible. The planet had no atmosphere; there was no pressure outside. Despite this, three areas lost integrity. We were open to the elements. I staggered to my feet and overrode the comms.

'Emergency! We have a hull breach!'

I heard Danny's voice. He was frantic. 'What section?'

'Evacuate 11 to 13. The base is open! Repeat, the base is open!'

If we lost more than a third of the oxygen in the base, we'd never replenish it before we all suffocated.

I needed to get Doors 10 and 14 shut. On a monitor, I could see Danny was with the new arrivals in Ood Habitation.

'Get out of there, Danny!'

For a moment, he looked lost. The Doctor grabbed him by the arm and dragged him towards the door. The girl, Rose Tyler, was already heaving the wheel open on Door 20. The Doctor and Rose worked together instinctively. Calm, no panic. A team. But, despite their efforts, they weren't going to make it. We were losing oxygen at a greater rate than they could run. Ood Habitation was on the far side of the base. If I waited until they made it all the way to Door 38 and safety, there wouldn't be enough oxygen left for any of us.

I was going to have to sacrifice them. What choice did I have?

I saw that Jefferson had reached Door 38 and had wedged himself in the frame to keep it open against the howling gale of escaping air. Ida and the last of the security detail made it through thanks to him.

'Come on!' Jefferson reached through the door and pulled Toby by the arm. 'And you, sunshine, come on!' He looked up at the camera above the door. 'How many more, Zack?' he yelled at me, the comms channel distorting as the wind throttled the mics.

It should have been Jefferson who stepped up when the Captain died, not me. He was older, more experienced. He'd spent his life in deep space. But the chain of command said otherwise, and now it was up to me to make the decision to sacrifice three lives to save everyone else. Did I have it in me to order Jefferson to get out of the way, so I could close the door and condemn Danny and the new arrivals to death? How would I face Jefferson afterwards? How would I face myself?

An alert sounded on the console. The drill was drifting from its target. The computer was struggling to maintain the position of the force fields that were keeping the drill vertical.

And that was the moment I realised I could save them. We'd cannibalised the ship's force fields to stabilise the drill, but why couldn't I use the fields to hold the atmosphere in place – at least until Danny and the others were through? Force fields operated by interacting with an object's mass. All I had to do was calibrate a force field strong enough to contain the atmosphere, but porous enough for Danny and the others to run through. In a few seconds, it was in place. On my screen, I watched Jefferson look around him, puzzled, as the wind dropped, but the air remained.

He looked up at the camera. 'What's going on, Zack? Are we out of air?'

As I explained what I'd done, Danny, the Doctor and Rose dived through the door, and Jefferson slammed it shut behind them, spinning the locking wheel.

There was sudden quiet. Alone on the command deck, cold sweat trickled down my back. Over the comms, I could hear the gasps of the crew as they sucked down oxygen. Only the Doctor seemed unaffected.

'Everyone all right?' he asked, calmly. 'What happened? What was it?'

'Hull breach,' Jefferson replied, still taking gasps of air. 'We were open to the elements. Two more minutes, and we'd have been inspecting that Black Hole at close quarters.'

'That wasn't a quake,' I heard the Doctor say. 'What caused it?'

'We've lost Sections 11 to 13,' I said, cutting him off quickly. It wasn't the time for a debrief, I needed to know that everyone was all right. When Jefferson told me that we had everyone except Scooti, I remembered her earlier distress and was hit by a wave of dread. I brought up a schematic of the base and activated her tracker. We'd all had them implanted under our skin before the mission began. I relaxed when I saw a small light pulsing within the two-dimensional layout of the base.

I hit the comms. 'She's all right, I've found her biochip, she's in Habitation 3. She's not responding, she might be unconscious.' I sat back in my chair, exhausted. 'How about that? We survived.'

I was wrong.

Ida

Once the pressure in the base had stabilised, Jefferson led the party to find Scooti. I stayed back, crouched against a wall, sucking oxygen down into my lungs. The recycled air of the base had never felt so sweet. The Doctor and Rose were helping Toby to his feet. He didn't seem to know what had happened to him.

'I was working . . .' he murmured. 'And then . . . I can't remember. All that noise. The room was falling apart. There was no air . . .'

'Come on, up you get,' Rose said brightly. 'Come and have some Protein One.'

'You've gone native,' the Doctor grinned, grabbing Toby's other arm to steady him.

'Hey, don't knock it,' Rose replied. 'It's nice, Protein One, with a little bit of Three.'

As they supported him along the walkway, Toby was staring at his hands, as if he might find the answer to something there. It occurred to me at the time that he was losing it, that being out here had been too much for someone as brittle and arrogant as him.

We would find out to our cost that Toby's problems weren't in his head.

When we entered Habitation 3, Toby shrugged off the Doctor and Rose's help and went and sat down.

Jefferson turned to me, concern on his face. 'There's no sign of her, but her biochip says she's in this area.' He called over to Toby, 'Were you with her? Did you see Scooti?'

Toby was staring at the floor. He shook his head but didn't look up.

I called her on the comms, but no joy. It was possible her tracker was malfunctioning. You couldn't rely on any tech on the base. Jefferson informed Zack that she was still missing, but he was adamant that Scooti's biochip was registering as being in Habitation 3.

'That's where I am,' Jefferson insisted, 'and I'm telling you, she's not here.'

Behind me, somebody spoke. Their voice was almost a whisper; so low I didn't recognise who it was.

'I've found her.' The Doctor was staring up at the observation window in the roof.

'Oh my god!' Rose exclaimed.

Scooti wasn't in Habitation 3. She was above it. Floating above us in the zero gravity of space. She looked as if she were underwater, her hair floating around her face. Her eyes were open, staring down at us, blankly. Her left hand was raised. It looked, horribly, as if she were waving at us.

Beside me, the Doctor whispered, 'I'm sorry. I'm so sorry,' as if it had been his responsibility to keep her alive. I felt a wave of anger at his presumption. He'd barely said two words to her. I was the one who knew her! I was the one who'd befriended her, when it was clear that she was less experienced than she'd let on. I was the one who'd listened to her late at night, when she confessed she was homesick for her parents. Oh god, her parents, someone would have to tell them.

'She was twenty,' I found myself saying out loud. 'She was twenty years old.'

Above us, her slender body began to twist away, the Black Hole exerting itself over her.

As we lost her to the darkness, Jefferson quoted something from memory: 'For how can man die better, than facing fearful odds, For the ashes of his father, and the temples of his Gods.'

The author was Macaulay. I didn't know it at the time. I tracked it down later. I've read Macaulay often in the weeks since I've got back and, when I do, I think of Scooti, and of Jefferson. Scooti wasn't the only one who faced fearful odds, nor was she the only one who didn't make it back.

For a long moment, no one spoke. I realised there was a new quality to the quiet.

'It's stopped.'

'What has?' Rose asked.

The Doctor put his hands in his pockets. 'The drill.'

We'd done it. The drill had reached penetration point. We were there.

Zack looked shaken when I joined him in the command centre, so I slipped my arm around him. We reviewed the security footage leading up to the depressurisation in silence. A window had blown out of the section Scooti was in. Just before she died, she'd been staring out of it, looking distressed. There was no footage of what she was looking at. All the external cameras were directed inwards to assess damage caused by the quakes. The planet was so much rock – why look out? The audio on the recording was damaged, but Zack had heard her over the comms say, 'It's not possible' and 'You can't be'. Thankfully the camera went down when the atmosphere blew out. I didn't want to see her last moments.

Had she seen something out there? Or had she just lost the plot? After eight months, we were all feeling strung out, and she and Toby were the most fragile, but that didn't explain the base's loss of integrity. Where had that overwhelming pressure come from? The external windows were designed to withstand a direct hit from a meteorite. What could have cracked that reinforced glass?

Zack shrugged. 'None of it makes sense. Not the loss of integrity, not the drill.'

I nodded. 'It's way ahead of schedule.'

'It's like the rock just gave way.'

'We've got to go down,' I said.

He hesitated before replying. 'I think we should be cautious.'

I suspected this was coming. Zack was facing the first major decision of his command. It was his decision whether we continued, or packed up and went home with our tails between our legs. 'Scooti worked in Engineering,' I told him. 'She welded half that drill head together. What would she say now? Come on, Zack. People died to get us this far. Don't abandon them now.'

The Doctor, Rose and Danny arrived before Zack could give his answer, so I had to endure Danny babbling away about the Ood of all things. For some inexplicable reason, he wanted them locked up.

'I think we should contain them ...' he hissed, glancing over at the couple of Ood that were conducting maintenance on the other side of the room.

Zack wasn't having it. 'We need them on the mineshaft,' he hissed back, before catching himself. 'What am I whispering for? They're just Ood, for god's sake!'

I was surprised when Rose agreed with Danny. He was an anxious kid, always jumping at his own shadow, but Rose struck me as being made of sterner stuff. 'You should listen to him,' she insisted. 'Something's wrong with them.'

Zack was looking past her, frowning. 'Do you mind?'

The Doctor looked up from where he had unscrewed a control panel. He grinned, caught out.

'I thought it might be useful to have an audio link to the drill head.'

Zack was nonplussed. 'It's a mineshaft on a dead planet, what's there to listen to?'

'Well, let's find out. The drill's got automatic receptors – it's just a case of waking them up.'

He pointed the little device he carried around with him. It gave an annoying insect buzz and the speakers on the console came to life with a crackle. The room filled with a familiar but chilling sound. A low thump, repeating itself. Two thumps in fact, one immediately after the other. A heartbeat. Huge. Echoing. Like a giant in a cave.

Rose hugged herself. 'That's coming from … down … there?'

Nothing had descended to the depths of the planet for millions of years. There was no air, no light. How could anything be alive?

The Doctor turned to Zack, his eyes sparkling with excitement. 'We've so got to go down there.'

A moment ago, I'd been trying to persuade Zack of the same thing, now I wasn't so sure. Nor, it seemed, was Zack.

'I haven't made my decision. It's clear Toby's not in any state to …'

The Doctor interrupted him. 'I volunteer! Right here and now. Put me down for the expedition, sir!'

'That would be breaking every protocol in the book. We don't even know who you are.'

'Yes, but you trust me, don't you?' the Doctor asked, with a knowing grin. 'Go on, look me in the eye. Yes, you do. I can see it. Right there. Trust.'

Zack couldn't hold his gaze. 'It should be me going down there.'

I wondered if the Doctor was going to call him out for his cowardice, but instead, he spoke softly. 'The captain doesn't lead the mission. He stays here, in charge. That's the job.'

'Not much good at it, am I?' Zack turned to the console and activated the comms. 'Prepare for descent. I repeat. Prepare for descent. T minus one hour.'

When I looked back at the Doctor, he was staring right at me. I wondered if he could read me as easily as he did Zack.

'What do you say, Ida?'

What else could I say?

My hands were trembling as I pulled on the environment suit. I whispered the safety checklist as I did: oxygen, nitrobalance, sealant, magnetic soles. I hesitated before pulling on the goldfish bowl helmet. Once it was on, I would be committed to going down into the darkness to face ... what? Whatever had that pulsing heartbeat in its chest.

The drill sight had been cleared of mining equipment. Despite Danny's insistence that the Ood all be confined to Ood Habitation, Zack had authorised three to be kept in service. They were using a portable crane to attach the lift capsule to the winch. The Doctor and I were going to be reliant on a single steel cable to lower us to whatever was down there. And, hopefully, to bring us back up.

Over the rim of my suit, I watched Rose approach the Doctor. She had a brave smile on her face, but the way she jammed her hands in her pockets betrayed her fears.

'S'funny,' she started, 'cos I get spoilt with you. I thought space travel was all, sort of ... TARDISes and whizzing about and Captain Jack, y'know, like it's fun. But it's not, is it? It's tough.'

They looked at each other for a long moment, before the Doctor fastened his helmet in place. 'I'll see you later.' He spoke with such certainty that for a moment I relaxed, confident that we would return, but it wasn't a promise he could make.

'Not if I see you first,' Rose joked. She stood up on tiptoe and kissed his visor.

The Doctor turned to me. 'Ready?'

No, I thought to myself, but I made my way to the lift all the same. I'd been to a dozen planning meetings about the capsule itself, but none of them had prepared me for how primitive it felt once I was inside. It was little more than an open cage made of steel struts and a metal floor, painted construction yellow. I told myself that simple was better; less that could go wrong. The capsule swung alarmingly as Jefferson operated the controls to raise it from the floor and move it over the borehole. I caught a glimpse of the rough, rock walls of the borehole, disappearing down into the darkness beneath us. My stomach lurched.

With the grinding of gears, we started to descend. Jefferson gave me a reassuring nod as we disappeared into the ground – and then there was only the rock wall of the borehole. The base receded to a circle of light above us, and then it shrank to a dot, then a faint glow, before it disappeared altogether. I felt as if I were drowning, and I swallowed down a desire to scream at Jefferson to throw the winch into reverse and bring us back up. The only light came from inside the suit helmets. The Doctor's face appeared to be floating in space in front of me.

What the hell was I doing? What questionable series of decisions had brought me to this moment? The darkness brought a clarity. I hadn't decided to come out to the edge of known space for adventure or scientific advancement. I'd been running away from my life. The late Captain's mission had simply been a convenient way to put as much distance between myself and home as possible. An image of my father in his hospital bed came unwelcome to my mind: his skeletal arms reaching out for me, his claw-like fingers finding only air. He had needed me and I'd run away. The consequence of my cowardice had left me deep in the heart of a dead planet, below the most destructive power in the universe.

Zack's voice came over the comms, interrupting my musings. 'You've gone beyond the oxygen field. You're on your own.'

The Doctor nimbly switched over to the oxygen tank on his back and I followed suit. The dusty air of the tank flooded my helmet. I held on to a breath until the urge to cough left me. Any phlegm I brought up would coat the inside of my visor for the rest of the mission.

Rose's voice came over the comms. 'Don't forget to breathe. Breathing is good.'

'Rose, stay off the comms,' Zack exclaimed, exasperated.

'No chance,' Rose replied, unabashed.

Beside me, the Doctor smiled to himself.

I couldn't imagine the circumstances that had brought the Doctor and Rose together – they were such different people – but what kept them together was obvious. They were incredibly brave, throwing themselves into whatever situation they found themselves in. As the Doctor and I descended ever downwards, I wished I had a little of their *joie de vivre*.

There was a hideous screech of metal, and the capsule shuddered. I made a grab for the safety rail but missed. I lost my balance and would have hit the ground, but suddenly the Doctor's hands were gripping my upper arms.

'You're okay, I've got you,' he murmured. 'The borehole is uneven. Shards from the drill. It's not the smoothest way to get to a planet's core.'

What other ways were there? I wondered. But not for long. One moment I was on my feet, the next I was flat on my back. My helmet slammed against the floor of the capsule, and the back of my head cracked forcefully against it. White hot pain shot through me. I instinctively went to cradle my head, but my gloved hands met the glass helmet. I fought an urge to throw up. Voices joined the agony in my mind.

'Doctor? Doctor, are you all right?' Rose's voice was full of anxiety.

'Ida?' Zack was professional, but just as concerned. 'Report to me. Ida? Report!'

I couldn't speak for fear of losing control over the contents of my stomach.

I heard the Doctor's voice: 'We're all right.'

Were we? I opened my eyes. The Doctor certainly seemed to be. He was crouched over me, his face a soft blue from the internal light in his helmet.

'We've made it.'

I lifted myself onto the padded elbow of my suit. My visor was misted up. All I could see was the yellow frame of the capsule and beyond that ... blackness. The Doctor hooked his hands under the armpits of my suit and heaved me to my feet. He was surprisingly strong despite his skinny frame. I stepped out of the lift onto uneven stone ground. Loose rocks skittered under my feet, forcing me to scurry down to a flatter area. I glanced back at the capsule. It had come to rest by the wall of what I assumed was some sort of cavern. The light from my torch lit up the cavern floor for twenty or so yards, but how far it stretched beyond that, I couldn't see.

I called to the Doctor to bring a gravity globe from the capsule. He tossed it over to me and I caught it as Rose came over the comms.

'What's it like down there?'

The Doctor frowned and waved his torch through the air. 'Hard to tell. Some sort of cave. Massive.'

'This should help,' I said and depressed the control stud on the base of the globe. It started to glow and push against my hands, wanting to rise. Before it grew too bright, I swung it up, high above us, where it bounced gently on the air, before coming to rest, close to the cavern's roof, and exploding with light.

Massive was an understatement. And it was clear straight away that this wasn't a natural cavern. Huge stone statues of animals stared down at us, their faces stylised wolves, cats and birds. Gods that had once been worshipped? Or sentinels to scare off the unworthy?

The sides of the cavern had been carved into smooth vertical walls, which boasted bridges and balconies. People – or creatures that had lived like people – had walked through this place. Had they worshipped here or come for some other purpose at which we could only guess? A giant fissure at the far end of the cavern led to bridges that spanned a tall waterfall. Who had brought water down here? And how? The entire structure required a technology that was beyond our imagining.

But then, wasn't that why we had come? I just hadn't expected it to be so beautiful.

Next to me, the Doctor was looking around us, with the same awe I was feeling. 'Rose,' he said into the comms, 'you can tell Toby that we've found his civilisation.'

Her reply came back immediately. 'Hey Toby, sounds like you've got plenty of work coming up.'

The microphone on Rose's communicator picked up Toby's voice. He mumbled his reply, which I didn't make out, but I was too focused on my new surroundings to care. I must've laughed in wonder because the next thing I heard was Zack's voice in my ear.

'Concentrate now, people, keep on the mission. Ida, what about the power source?'

In the thrill of discovery, I had forgotten that this whole enterprise was essentially a salvage operation. We were really here to scavenge for whatever the ancient civilisation had left behind. The energy reading on my wrist-com was off the scale. 'We're close, energy signature indicates north north-west. You getting pictures up there?'

'Too much interference,' Zack replied in my ear. 'We're in your hands.'

Despite all that we'd lost to arrive here, my anxieties evaporated in the excitement of discovery. I started to follow the reading to the source of the energy signal. 'We've come this far, no turning back.'

'Oh, did you have to?' the Doctor exclaimed, next to me. '"No turning back," that's almost as bad as "Nothing can possibly go wrong." Or "It's gonna be the best Christmas Walford's ever had."'

I stared at him, bemused by his references and, not for the first time, wondering where the hell he came from. 'Have you finished?'

He looked a little sheepish. 'I've finished.'

The energy reading led us to the far side of the temple. It was simpler here; fewer structures carved into the walls and no statues. The cavern walls were rough and unfinished, as if whoever built this place didn't want to hang around to finish the job properly. But what we were looking for wasn't on the walls.

It was on the ground.

'We've found something,' the Doctor said into his comms. I could almost feel the team's anticipation above us. The Doctor described it better than I could. 'It's like bronze, like some sort of seal, or ... I've got a nasty feeling the word might be "trapdoor". Not a good word, trapdoor. I've never met a trapdoor I liked.'

I knelt down at its edge, which was slightly below the level of the cavern floor, like a stopper forced into a bottle. 'It's covered in those symbols.'

'Do you think it opens?' Zack asked over the comms.

'That's what trapdoors tend to do,' the Doctor murmured unhappily.

'Trapdoor doesn't do it justice, Zack,' I said. 'It's massive, like the door to a vault, only built into the floor.'

'Any way of opening it?'

'Don't know, I can't see any mechanism.'

The Doctor crouched down next to me, to get a better view. 'I suppose that's the writing. It would tell us what to do. The letters that defy translation.'

I asked Zack if Toby had made any progress with decoding the symbols we'd found during the drilling. I heard him instruct Toby to report in, but Toby didn't reply. We didn't know then that Toby wasn't taking instructions any more.

At least, he wasn't taking them from us.

Danny

If Zack had taken me seriously, he wouldn't have allowed three of the Ood to assist with the capsule's descent. The truth was he couldn't see the Ood as a threat, but then he hadn't seen what I'd seen. Oh, he seconded Martin from Jefferson's maintenance and security detail for my protection, but what could one person do if the entire Ood population turned on us? They outnumbered us five to one!

I'd never really got on with Martin. He was part of Jefferson's crew. He drank with Curt and Chenna; military types who spent their downtime engaging in target practice in the drilling area. Our relationship wasn't helped when he'd briefly dated Scooti soon after we arrived. He knew I liked her and checked that I was fine with him asking her out, as he 'didn't want to step on anyone's toes'. So patronising. It didn't help that he asked me in front of everyone. Scooti laughed and told him not to be silly, before slipping her arm into his and disappearing off to his room for the night.

I wondered how he felt about her death. He didn't seem affected by it. He stood next to me, looking bored as he worked off a smudge of grease on the barrel of his firearm. He looked like he wanted to be anywhere but here, although, to be fair, no one volunteered to work in the Ood Pen.

Down below us, the Ood sat on their benches facing one another. At least a dozen of them were housed in this section. They sat, motionless in the shadows. You wouldn't have known they were there, if it weren't for the faint odour of the reptile house that drifted up from the gloom.

I diverted the comms channel through the speakers on my console, so we could hear the mission's progress. Ida and the Doctor's tinny voices filled the pen. Martin didn't show much interest in the capsule's descent, which did make me wonder why he'd ventured all the way out here in the first place. I heard the capsule arrive at its destination. The sound of its impact almost blew the monitors. There was a flurry of chatter on the comms as everyone talked over each other.

Something caught my attention in my peripheral vision, making the hairs on the back of my neck stand up. At the moment the capsule had reached its target, all the Ood in the pen had stood up. Now they turned to face us. They were looking up at us, impassive. I ordered them to return to their previous positions, but they didn't move.

I opened a channel to Zack. 'Captain, it's happening again – the Ood.'

'What are they doing?'

'They're staring at me.' I winced as I heard Zack exhale with irritation, but I pressed on. 'I've told them to stop, but they won't.'

'Danny, you're a big boy, I think you can take being stared at.'

On my terminal screen, I saw that the Ood's telepathic field was, quite literally, off the charts. I ran a quick diagnostic, but it wasn't an error. The telepathic field was at Basic 100. I informed the Captain, and he stated the obvious.

'That's impossible.'

It was. Over the comms, I heard Jefferson tell Rose that Basic 100 meant brain death. Zack asked me if the Ood were doing anything. When I told him they weren't, he ordered me to keep watching them.

What else was I going to do?

Zack told Jefferson to assign one of his team to monitor the three Ood that were still working the drill site.

'Officer. At arms,' Jefferson instructed a nearby officer.

'You can't fire a gun in here,' Rose exclaimed. 'What if you hit the wall?'

'It's Firing Stock 15, only impacts upon organics.'

The Doctor's voice came over the comms. 'Everything all right up there?' From the concern in his voice, he hadn't missed the gun talk.

'Yeah!' Rose responded brightly.

'Fine!' said Zack.

I was about to add my own words of reassurance, when Martin tugged at my arm. He was staring down into the pen. Below us, the Ood had climbed to their feet, still looking up at us. As one they began to move, single file, up the stairs towards us. I ordered them to sit back down, but they ignored me. Martin brought his firearm to bear on them.

'Let's get out of here.'

'Why?' Martin shrugged, taking aim. 'It's not like they're armed.'

As he finished speaking, the nearest Ood reached the top of the stairs. And then – almost faster than I could see – its translator globe leapt from its hand and attached itself to Martin's forehead. There was the crackle of energy, the smell of burnt flesh and Martin was flung on his back. His eyes open, sightless.

He was dead.

I stared at Martin's murderer, unable to compute what had just happened. The Ood were conditioned creatures. Like the androids of the past, they were programmed to assist human beings, not hurt them. It should have been impossible for them to attack a crew member, let alone kill them.

I backed away from the advancing Ood, eyeing its communicator globe, which was floating slowly in the air between us, like a cobra preparing to strike.

Zack's voice came over the comms, asking Toby for a progress report on his translation of the symbols. When he didn't get an answer, Rose pushed him for one. 'They need to know – that lettering, does it make any sense?'

As Toby replied, the comms started to break up. I managed to catch one word in three.

'*These . . . words . . . beast . . .*'

It was Toby's voice, but it didn't sound like him. It was lower, more intense. His tone put my nerves on edge.

And then around me, the Ood chorused:

'*He is the heart that beats in the darkness, the blood that will never cease. And now he will rise.*'

The comms distorted with the sound of Jefferson yelling something at Toby. I thought I heard gunfire. The link to the drill room suddenly died. The Ood began to move forward, stepping over Martin's body as if it were a minor inconvenience. I turned and fled.

The base was deserted as I raced to the drill site. I kept imagining seeing Ood around every corner, but the others must have still been obeying orders. The crew were either at the command centre or the drill site. I managed to get to the door to the drill site and feverishly spun the wheel. The ten seconds it took to open were the longest of my life. If the Ood attacked now, I'd be trapped. The smell of Martin's burnt flesh was still in my nostrils. How could an Ood kill? It was insane.

When the door finally opened, I realised I'd been holding my breath. I leapt through and ordered the computer to close the door. There was an agonising wait, before I could spin the wheel and lock it.

'It's the Ood, they've gone mad,' I shouted as I locked the door behind me. 'They killed Martin!'

Only then did I turn my attention to the raised voices in the drill room. Jefferson was on the far side of the borehole. He was sweating, his face flushed with emotion. He'd raised his firearm and was taking aim at someone with their back to me. Despite not being able to see his face, I could see it was Toby. There was something defiant about the boy's stance.

The comms were still operational here. The Doctor's voice was broadcasting over it, tinny and urgent. 'What is it? What's he done? What's happening? Rose? What's going on?'

Rose was by Jefferson's side, staring in horror at Toby. Before she could reply, Zack overrode the channel from the control centre. 'Jefferson! Report!'

Jefferson wasn't listening. He cocked his firearm, ready to fire. His face was set. His shirt drenched in sweat. He meant it. He was going to shoot Toby!

'Officer, this is your last chance,' he said, a tremor in his voice. 'You will stand down and confine yourself immediately.'

Toby drew himself up to his full height. He made a show of cracking his neck, as if he were gearing up for a bar fight. 'Mr Jefferson. Tell me, sir. Did your wife ever forgive you?' Toby sounded as if he were speaking from deep within a huge chamber. I wanted to see his face, to understand how he was speaking like this, but he didn't turn to look at me.

'I don't know what you mean,' Jefferson stammered, which was clearly a lie.

'Let me tell you a secret. She never did.'

What was Toby playing at? Whatever it was, Jefferson didn't like it. He brought his gun up to his eye and stared down the target. 'You will stand down or be confined.'

'Or what?'

'Under the strictures of Condition Red, I'm authorised to shoot you.'

This was too much. I shouted at Jefferson to put the gun down. 'It's Toby for Chrissakes!'

At the sound of my voice, Toby turned to face me. I took an involuntary step back. His face was covered in the symbols he'd spent the last eight months researching. My first thought was that he'd drawn them onto his face, but when I looked more closely I realised with horror that they were burnt into his skin. Had he done that to himself? And then I noticed his eyes. They were bright red and flickered with a fire from within.

I'd been wrong. This wasn't Toby. This was someone else.

Some*thing* else.

Toby turned back to Jefferson. 'You can try and shoot me. But how many can you kill?'

Toby arched his back and yelled in pain. I couldn't see his face, but black smoke started to escape from it. Was he burning up? The smoke drifted across the drill site towards the three Ood that Zack had allowed to continue to work. It was only then that

I realised the smoke wasn't drifting, it was moving purposefully towards them. They sucked the strange smoke through their mandibles, swallowing it down into their lungs. One after the other they shivered as if the smoke were a drug taking effect. One of them turned to look at me, its eyes now burning with the same scarlet fire as Toby's. Whatever had taken possession of him now had control of the Ood.

'We are the Legion of the Beast.'

It raised its communication globe, which was burning with a bright white light. Its fellows followed suit. Over the comms, I heard other Ood throughout the base join in a chant.

'The Legion will be many, and the Legion shall be few. We shall stand as sentinels for his awakening to herald his arrival to their world.'

It was all of them. All of the Ood were possessed! But with what? Or whom?

The Doctor's voice came over the comms. 'Rose, what is it? Rose? I'm coming back up!'

Ida

The Doctor turned from the giant, levelled disk and sprinted towards the far side of the cavern where the capsule stood, leaning awkwardly on the cavern floor. As he ran, the ground began to tremble beneath us, rubble rumbled as it bounced on the uneven ground.

'Doctor! Wait!' I shouted as I began to chase after him.

Events were moving too quickly to process. Moments ago, the crew's focus had been on us, on what we had discovered at the bottom of the borehole. Now the crisis that was unfolding above us had left us forgotten. How was it possible that the Ood had gone haywire? If we'd lost control of them, we'd lost control of the base. We could barely operate it with them; if they'd turned against us, we'd be at their mercy. I tried to keep my feet as I raced after the Doctor, whilst the Ood's words echoed in my head:

'The Legion stand as sentinels for his awakening to herald his arrival in this world.'

I wasn't an anthropologist; that was Toby's department. But the words of the Ood sounded somehow generic. All kinds of broadcasts were drawn to the Black Hole. For all we knew the Ood might have picked up a few stray sentences from a fictional story broadcast hundreds of years ago. The real question was – why did they believe it? Had the malfunction of the telepathic field left them vulnerable to suggestion? Had they become religious zealots due to a random broadcast and a fluctuation in their brain waves?

As an explanation, it felt implausible. But the alternative was unthinkable.

The tremors had increased in intensity by the time the Doctor entered the capsule and slammed the cage door behind him. Above him, the quake was causing the cable to snake and slam against the cavern wall. I grabbed the cage door and yanked it back open.

'You can't go back up!' I yelled over the rumbling of the quake.

In the shadows of the lift, the Doctor's eyes were bright with fear. Not for himself, but for his friend. 'Rose is up there.'

'The tremors will smash the capsule to pieces if you try to take it up.' As if to prove my point, the cable hit the cavern wall with such violence that a shower of rock tumbled to the ground around us.

The Doctor pulled me under the shelter of the capsule roof. When he spoke, his face was right up against mine. 'I brought her here. It's bad enough

I can't get her home, but I won't abandon her. I can't.'

'You can't help her if you're dead. And you'd be killing me too, because this is the only way out.'

I felt his body sag with resignation. He knew I was right. He activated the comms. 'Rose! Jefferson! What is going on up there?'

The voice that replied was neutral, calm and inhuman.

'*Since the dawn of time, he has woven himself through the fabric of your life; some may call him Abaddon, some may call him Krop Tor, some may call him Satan or Lucifer or the King of Despair, the Deathless Prince, the Bringer of Night.*'

Krop Tor? This was no stray broadcast picked up by the Ood's telepathic field. This was the mythology of the Black Hole. A shard of icy terror slid into my guts. It was impossible. Creatures from religious mythology did not suddenly announce themselves – the idea was too ridiculous to contemplate – but that was exactly what it had done. More than that, it had said it was all of them. Every devil or demon – every destroyer from every religion – every flip side of a benevolent creator myth.

Something nagged at me. A conversation from years before. Something about the myth of Krop Tor.

Then everything changed.

A terrible grinding sound reverberated through the cavern. I had to cover my ears as the sound of metal on metal shrieked around us. A new voice joined the Ood over the comms. Low, silken, knowing:

'I am become manifest. I shall walk in the light. And my legions will swarm across the worlds.'

'The trapdoor!' the Doctor exclaimed.

We retraced our steps as quickly as we could. Rocks fell from the ceiling. One of them hit the gravity globe and sent it careering around the cavern, its light flickering through the falling debris. The ground shifted beneath us. When I fell to my knees, the Doctor ran back and grabbed my arm and led me through the darkness.

And still the voice taunted me in my ears. *'The time of the new is passed, and I shall rise, as the Old One restored and sanctified in blood.'*

'Doctor!' I cried out, pointing at the trapdoor. 'It's opening!'

The metal disk was retracting, sections of it folding in on themselves, revealing only darkness below.

'I am the sin, and the temptation, and the desire. I am the pain and the loss and the death of hope.'

And then from below, down in the depths – the heartbeat. Huge, echoing through the chamber. It was down there, in the darkness, waiting.

The Devil itself.

Danny

The voice was broadcasting on all channels of the communication system. We had no way of reaching Zack or Ida and the Doctor. Rose grabbed my hand to drag me away from the three Ood that advanced on us, their eyes burning red. We ducked behind Jefferson, who was the only one of us who was armed. The Ood were blocking the only exit from the drill site. There was no way to escape them.

Rose's hand felt soft and warm in mine, but I wasn't going to kid myself that it was a romantic gesture. She was trying to save my life. When I told Jefferson to shoot the Ood, Rose snatched her hand out of mine.

'You can't,' she snapped, shocked.

'They killed Martin, they're homicidal.'

'It's not them. They're being controlled.'

Before I could reply, the ground lurched beneath us and the base creaked and groaned. It felt like it was being torn apart.

I tried the comms again: 'Zack, what's happening?'

Zack

The regulations were clear. During a crisis, the captain never leaves the command centre. To do so could endanger the entire expedition. So I had to sit tight whilst Ida and a complete stranger undertook the mission that had brought us out here. I had to sit tight whilst the Ood overrode their conditioning and attacked the people they were supposed to be serving. I had to act calm and in control while an unknown entity took possession of Toby.

It wasn't easy to sit on my hands whilst my crewmates faced danger. But when a new alarm began to sound in the command centre, I realised why someone had to stay at the helm. There were so many alarms already sounding that I almost didn't notice it at first. I had only ever heard it being tested. I'd hoped that would be the only time I would hear it.

The gravity field was failing.

I rechecked the detectors, but the readings were unequivocal – a gravitational force of exceptional power was being enacted upon the base and the planet it rested upon. The Black Hole was drawing us in.

'We're moving!' I yelled over the shuddering tremors. 'The whole thing's moving, the planet's moving!'

We had travelled all this way with no understanding of the ancient mechanism that exempted this world from one of the fundamental laws of the universe. But now the Black Hole was finally recognising the planet's mass, gravity was folding around us and starting to draw us in. The hungry god was making another attempt at swallowing the bitter pill that it had once spat out. And this time it was going to swallow us down with it.

I tried to get Ida on the comms, but the Ood's religious rants were blocking every channel. Then a new voice suddenly joined the chorus:

'I have been imprisoned for all eternity, but no more. The Pit is open and I am free.'

Danny

When I heard the gravity field was failing, I don't know how I didn't give up then and let the three

Ood finish me off. I'd seen how they'd killed Martin; death would be instantaneous if not painless. But I didn't give up. I wouldn't. Perhaps life is so precious that we'll do anything to preserve one more second of it, even if there's no hope of survival.

As the Ood walked calmly towards us, their deadly communicators floating in the air in front of them, I yelled at Jefferson to open fire. The clatter of bullets filled the air, deafening me as the Ood were flung to the ground. Blood oozed from bullet holes in their work fatigues. I'd never seen an Ood wounded before.

Their blood was red, just like ours.

Next to me, Rose was yelling at Jefferson. I couldn't hear what she was saying for the ringing in my ears, but the force with which she pushed Jefferson in the chest left me in no doubt that she was expressing her fury at what he had just done.

What I had encouraged him to do.

Zack's voice came over the comms as the tremors subsided. 'We're stabilising. The gravity field's holding, we've got orbit!'

The sweat cooled on my skin. My pulse slowed. The ringing in my ears receded. There was silence in the drill area. The Ood's blood looked *very* red in the brightness of the overhead lights. Rose turned to look at me, disgust on her face. Any hope that she might like me in the way I liked her evaporated in that moment. I was relieved when she turned away and tried to reach the Doctor on the comms.

Adrenalin had left a bitter taste in the back of my mouth. I felt nauseous. Unsure what to do with myself, I joined Jefferson at a security screen, which showed half a dozen Ood standing outside the door. We weren't going anywhere.

'I've got very little ammunition, sir,' Jefferson told Zack over the comms. 'What about you?'

The Captain's face replaced the Ood on the screen. There was sweat on his brow. 'All I've got is a bolt gun,' Zack replied, looking grim. He checked the chamber of the bolt gun, which, despite its name, looked more like something you'd find on a workman's belt than a weapon. 'With, uh, all of one bolt. I could take out a grand total of one Ood. Fat lot of good that is.'

'Given the emergency, sir, I'd recommend ... Strategy Nine.'

On screen, Zack nodded. 'I don't see an alternative. I tried to get out of the command centre, but I've got at least six of them outside.'

I coughed under my breath as I saw Rose was heading over to us. The last thing I wanted to do was to have to explain what Strategy Nine was. She focused her attention on Jefferson, not once looking in my direction. When she spoke, she was cold, businesslike.

'I can't get a reply from the Doctor. Are all communicators working?'

'They are up here,' Zack answered from the command centre.

'Then why can't I get through to the Doctor?'

None of us answered, but we were clearly all thinking the same thing. When the gravity field had failed, even for those few moments, the planet had shifted on its axis. Up here, the tremors had shaken us to our bones. What must it have done to Ida and the Doctor below us? They were in a cavern with a billion tons of rock above them.

I put my hand on Rose's shoulder. I was surprised when she didn't shrug it off.

Suddenly a chirpy voice interrupted the silence. 'No, sorry, we're fine, still here!'

At the sound of the Doctor's voice, Rose burst into a huge smile. She spun around, tangling herself up in the communicator cable, which responded with a squeal of feedback.

'Oh, you could've said, you stupid . . .'

Ida

The Doctor grimaced at the colourful language Rose called him for scaring her. 'Sorry,' he mouthed at me, as if, having survived almost falling into a black hole, I might be offended by swearing.

'Anyway! It's both of us, me and Ida, hello! But that seal opened up, it's gone, all we've got left is this ...' he searched for the right word. '... chasm.'

If 'trapdoor' was a worrying word, 'chasm' wasn't any more reassuring.

'How deep is it?' Zack asked.

'Can't tell. Looks like it goes on forever.'

Rose came back onto the comms. '"The Pit is open." That's what the voice said.'

'But there's nothing ...' Zack trailed off, as if uncertain how to express his thought. 'I mean, there's nothing coming out?'

'No.' The Doctor chuckled dryly. 'No sign of the Beast.'

There was a pause on the line before Rose rejoined with, 'It said it was Satan.'

'Come on, Rose,' the Doctor said, forcing a bright tone into his voice. 'Keep it together.'

'Is there no such thing?'

He didn't reply. I followed his gaze to the chasm beneath us.

'Doctor?' Rose's voice was urgent over the comms. 'Are you there? Doctor, tell me there's no such thing as Satan.'

For a long moment, all I could hear was the rise and fall of the ventilator in my suit. I couldn't take my eyes off the opening in the ground. Our borehole was rough and uneven – the capsule had sheared rock from the walls as we'd made our way down. Beneath the trapdoor, the walls of the pit shaft were smooth. Constructed. Someone had made it for a reason. Down there in the dark, something was alive. I'd heard its heartbeat. But the idea that someone had trapped the Devil down there was – what? Ridiculous seemed too small a word. Did anyone really believe in the Devil any more?

Once again, the legend of Krop Tor came unbidden to my mind and troubled my scientific reasoning. I'd never been bothered by religion. Growing up, there'd been none at home. My mother died of cancer, information she kept from us until her last weeks. And even on her morphine-drenched deathbed, she had been clear that goodbye meant exactly that. My father ... well, I don't know. I'm not sure I'm ready to talk about him. What I mean to say is, I grew up with what I felt was a healthy scepticism about the Devil and all its works. It seemed far more plausible that Lucifer's fall was a morality tale to socialise children than a description of some supernatural battle that actually took place.

As I trained as a physicist and then an astrophysicist, I had little need of faith. The more I explored the mechanism of the stars, the less troubled I was by religious explanations. It seemed clear to me that creation myths were pre-industrial species' attempts to make sense of what they could see and hear. Without meteorology, how else do you explain thunder and lightning? Gods with hammers fighting in the clouds seems as good an explanation as any. How could you possibly know that all that light and noise were electrical charge imbalances rapidly heating and expanding air? Religion's mistakes and misinterpretations suggested that its fountainheads were not supernatural entities, but all too fallible Earthly ones.

Which was why the Scriptures of the Veltino had always troubled me: 1,500 years before anyone had invented a telescope, let alone a gravitational wave detector, their scriptures described the Black

Hole above us as a hungry demon, tricked into devouring the planet only to spit it out because it was poison. Poetic, for sure. Metaphorical, certainly. But a hungry demon was undeniably a description of a black hole.

How could the authors of those scriptures have possibly known? If there was one religion in the universe that could claim to exhibit divine knowledge, it was this one.

And it was telling us in no uncertain terms that the Devil was real.

'Ida?' Zack interrupted my musings. 'I recommend that you withdraw, immediately.'

I felt relief that I could return to the surface, but also frustration. Had we really come all this way for nothing? Had Scooti?

'Sir, I really think—'

'Okay, that's an order,' Zack interrupted. 'Withdraw.'

'Zack, come on, we can't—'

'Listen, when that thing opened, the whole planet shifted – one more inch and we fall into the Black Hole. So this stops, right now.'

The more he spoke, the more reasonable he sounded, the more I wanted to find out what was down there.

'It's not like it's much better up there with the Ood,' I argued, certain now that I couldn't go home without answers.

'I'm initiating Strategy Nine, so I need the two of you back up top, immediately, no arguments.'

I deactivated the comms. One control on my wrist communicator and Zack's voice disappeared and with it, the chatter and hum of the Sanctuary Base above us. We were alone. The Doctor had a shocked expression on his face. I confess I was pleased to be able to surprise a man who had done nothing but surprise me since our first meeting.

'What do you think?' I asked him.

'He gave an order,' the Doctor replied gravely, but then he turned off his comms link as well.

'Yeah, but what do *you* think?'

He walked to the edge of the chasm and stood on the metal lip that had once framed the ancient covering. 'It said, *I am the temptation.*'

I joined him, the magnetic soles of my boots clanking as I stepped onto the metal rim. The darkness below us was impenetrable. 'If there's something down there ... why's it still hiding?'

The Doctor shrugged. 'Maybe we've opened the prison, but not the cell.'

I knew he was tempted to descend, find out what was there. I wasn't sure how much. And to be honest, I didn't want to go alone.

'We should go down,' I said. 'I'd go. What about you?'

The Doctor turned to me, a smile cracking across his face. 'Oh, in a second, but then again ...' He stopped and looked at me. No, he *appraised* me. 'That's so human. Where angels fear to tread. Even now, standing on the edge ... That feeling you get, yeah? Right at the back of your head, that impulse, that strange little impulse, that mad little voice saying, go on, go on, go over, go on ...'

We stood there, his words hanging between us, our feet standing on the very edge of the abyss. He was right. The impulse to go on, however dangerous or disastrous that might prove, was so strong.

As if he had heard the thought in my head, he said, 'Maybe it's relying on that. For once in my life, Officer Scott, I'm going to say ...'

He took a breath.

'Retreat.'

And then he exhaled. 'Now I *know* I'm getting old.' He stepped away from the edge and reactivated his comms link. 'Rose, we're coming back.'

Rose was delighted. 'Best news I've heard all day.'

'Ida?' the Doctor said. 'What's Strategy Nine?'

'Emergency protocol. Open the airlocks. We'll be safe inside a lockdown area. The Ood will get sucked out into the vacuum.'

'So we're going back to a slaughter?' His disapproval was like the shadow of a cloud blocking out the sun.

I shrugged. 'The Devil's work.'

I activated my comms and told Jefferson that we'd be ready to return in five minutes. We made our way back to the capsule, which was considerably easier now the ground was still. As we climbed into the capsule, I saw the Doctor glance back at the chasm.

'Now, don't look back. What was that old legend, Lot's wife and the pillar of salt?'

I could see he was still tempted to enter the Pit. We both were. I'd like to believe it was my scientific training – the noble pursuit of knowledge – but I think the Doctor was right: human beings can't help ourselves. Tell us not to touch the stove and there's always a little voice whispering, *How hot can it be?*

'Okay, we're in. Bring us up.'

I heard Jefferson start the ascent procedure. 'In three, two, one.'

The lights went out. The Doctor's face disappeared, leaving only an impression of his illuminated features on my vision. The ventilator on my suit wheezed and died. Fresh fear gripped my chest; I was going to suffocate ten miles below the surface.

'Doctor!'

'I'm here.'

I heard the familiar insect noise of the tool he carried around with him. The ventilator on my suit whirred back into life, rasping as it started to feed oxygen into my helmet. The monitor on the control console flickered once and then filled the capsule with soft blue light. The alien faces of the Ood crowded the screen. Their communicator globes floating in front of them, glowing brightly.

When they spoke, it was with that other voice: low, cunning, old.

'This is the darkness. This is my domain.'

I felt the Doctor's gloved hand take mine.

'You little things that live in the light. Clinging to your feeble suns which die in the end; they all die. Only the darkness remains.'

Zack's voice came over the comms. 'This is Captain Zachary Cross Flane of Sanctuary Base 6, representing the Torchwood Archive. You will identify yourself.'

'You know my name.'

'What do you want?'

'You will die here. All of you. This planet is your grave.'

Someone else's communicator must've picked up Toby's voice. Quiet, barely more than a whisper. 'It is, it's him, it's him.' He sounded broken, a lost soul.

The Doctor frowned. 'If you are the Beast, then answer me this. Which one? The universe has been busy since you've been gone, there's more religions than there are planets in the sky. The Arkiphets, Quoldonity, Christianity, Pash Pash, Neo-Judaism, San Claar, the Church of the Tin Vagabond ... Which devil are you?'

'All of them.'

'What, then ... ? You're the truth behind the myth?'

'This one knows me as I know him. The killer of his own kind.'

What the hell did that mean? I couldn't imagine the Doctor killing anyone. I expected the Doctor to defend himself, but he look startled, caught out. He changed his line of attack.

'How did you end up on this rock?'

'The Disciples of Light rose up against me, and chained me in the Pit for all eternity.'

Just a few moments ago, I had been thinking that Lucifer's Fall was a metaphor.

'When was this?' the Doctor demanded.

'Before Time.'

The Doctor scoffed. '"Before Time"? What does "Before Time" mean?'

'Before Time and Light and Space and Matter; before the cataclysm; before this universe was created.'

'That's impossible.' But the Doctor didn't sound as confident as he had a moment ago. 'No life could have existed back then.'

'Is that your religion?'

The Doctor's eyes widened, as if this thought had never occurred to him. He glanced at me, as if I might offer a response, but my throat was dry. Everything I knew was based on the observation that the Big Bang heralded the beginning of the universe, the beginning of Time itself. This creature was telling us that not only were the last fourteen billion years just a chapter of the story, but it had been there for the preceding part.

'It's a belief,' the Doctor finally replied.

'You know nothing. All of you, so small.'

It began to address us all. Revealing our most private thoughts.

'The Captain, so scared of command. The soldier, haunted by the eyes of his wife. The little boy who lied. The virgin. And the lost girl, so far away from home. The valiant child who will die in battle so very soon.'

I waited for it to address me, although I knew in my heart of hearts what it was going to say before it did.

'The scientist, still running from Daddy.'

If there really was a hell I was bound for, this was it.

Rose was shouting at the Doctor. She sounded desperate, but I could barely take in what she was saying.

'What does that mean?'

'Rose, don't listen!'

'What does that *mean*?'

While she demanded answers of the Doctor, I was back in the hospital with my father. The strong smell of disinfectant and the fainter smell of urine that it masked. Dementia had stolen the intelligence from his eyes, he was back in his childhood, crying for his mother who'd been dead for thirty years.

'You will die and I will live.'

The screen in the capsule flared and the image changed. The Ood were replaced – just for a moment – by a creature I recognised instantly. It was red and raging, white fangs against a horned face.

The Devil.

It was all true. Hell was real. And I'd burn for what I did.

The darkness was suddenly full of voices.

'Captain,' Jefferson barked, 'what's the situation with Strategy Nine? Captain, report?'

Zack didn't hear him. 'I've lost pictures, Mr Jefferson, have you got anything? Jefferson? You report to me!'

Their voices brought me out of the past. Reason asserted itself. A scientist doesn't take anyone's word for it, not even the word of some apparently omniscient creature. A scientist interrogates evidence.

I swallowed and cleared my throat. 'Did anyone get an analysis? Did we record that? Did we get biosigns? What's the readout?'

Everyone was speaking over one another. No one was listening. The main comms channel became a cacophony of panicked voices. Next to me, the Doctor grabbed a wired microphone from the wall of the capsule and turned up the gain until it squealed with feedback.

When he spoke, he was urgent but calm. 'If you want voices in the dark, then listen to mine. That thing is playing on very basic fears. Darkness, childhood, nightmare, all that stuff.'

'But that's how the Devil works,' Danny said. He sounded scared.

'Or a good psychologist.'

'How did it know about my father?' I said, unable to stop myself.

The Doctor turned to me. 'Okay,' he started, but I could see he didn't have an answer for that. He was thinking on his feet. It was what he did best: his thoughts and words forming at the same moment. 'But what makes his version of truth any better than mine? Cos I'll tell you what I can see. Humans. Brilliant humans. Humans who travelled all the way across space, flying in a tiny little rocket, right into the orbit of a black hole, just for the sake of discovery, that's amazing. Do you hear me? Amazing, all of you.' He fired his device at the images of the Ood on the monitor and they were replaced with the faces of Rose and the crew above us. 'The Captain. His officer. His elder. His junior. His friends. All with one advantage. The Beast is alone. We are not. If we can use that to fight against him . . .'

There was the sound of a distant explosion, and the comms went dead. A whispering, whipping sound grew above us. The cable had snapped. Ten miles of high-tensile wire was plummeting down towards us. Unaware, the Doctor was trying to reactivate the comms. I grabbed him by the arm and dragged him out of the capsule, running across the cavern and throwing us both to the ground.

The first part of the rope spooled around the capsule, kicking up dust and gravel. But the further it fell, the faster and harder it hit the ground. It snapped and lunged at us like an angry snake. We covered our heads with our hands, a useless gesture as the cable would slice our bodies in two if it landed on us. The sound of the cable hitting the ground built until suddenly it cut off. Had all the cable fallen? I opened my eyes and immediately they were filled with ancient grit. The air around us was opaque with dust that filled my mouth and throat. It felt like we were in the middle of a sandstorm. Above us the gravity globe hung like a desert sun. As the dust slowly settled, I saw why the noise of the falling rope had cut off so dramatically. The borehole was blocked with trapped cable, like worms in a can. There was no way back.

The Doctor had been wrong. We were on our own.

Danny

My hands were trembling as I ran a systems check. Life support was still functioning – we had air and heating. The emergency lighting kicked in, casting dark red shadows over the drill site. That creature had somehow severed the cable holding the lift capsule, trapping Ida and the Doctor ten miles below the surface. Separating us. What did the Devil want with us all? What were its plans for me?

'The boy who lied.' That had to be me. I wasn't married, a scientist or a virgin. Was I a liar? At first I couldn't think what it was referring to. My name really is Daniel Bartock. I hadn't misled anyone about my qualifications to join the mission. And then I realised what that horrific creature had meant, because my whole life was a lie. I'd lied at my job interview when I said I was interested in the mission, when all I'd wanted was a change of scene. What is reinvention but lying about who you are in order to be someone you'd rather be? I took this job because I thought it would offer me the chance to be someone other than the guy everyone tolerates, but secretly thinks is a bit of a joke. The guy that girls hang out with not because they like you, but because they think you're harmless.

That lie had got me here. Trapped between the Devil and a hungry god. And the irony was, I'd travelled all those light years to escape myself, only to discover I'd brought myself with me. I was still harmless Danny, who men teased and women patronised.

From nowhere, I felt a wave of rage. I'd show them . . .

I caught myself. Was that what it was doing? Illuminating our flaws so we'd turn on one another? I wasn't the only person who'd been humiliated by the Devil's words. Jefferson was shouting at Toby, his gun in his face. Toby was crouched in terror, covering his face with his arms.

Rose was trying to get between them, but Jefferson warded her away with his firearm.

'He's infected. He brought that thing into the base. You saw it!'

Rose wasn't having it. 'Are you going to shoot your own people, is that what you're going to do? Is it?'

'If necessary.'

Jefferson's face was flushed, there was a wildness in his eyes. He was smarting from what the creature had said to him, about how his wife had never forgiven him. Whatever he had done to her had shamed him to his core. And that shame was going to get Toby shot.

Rose stepped in front of Jefferson's gun. 'Then you'll have to shoot me,' she said coolly, fixing him with her steady brown eyes. 'So what's it going to be?'

The sweat on Jefferson's brow shone red in the emergency lights. He looked from where Toby cowered, and then back to Rose. Was he really capable of murder?

Rose capitalised on his hesitation. 'Look at his face. Whatever it was, it's gone, it passed into the Ood, you saw it happen. He's clean.'

I could see Jefferson didn't have a way to step down. He needed an off ramp, but there wasn't one.

I could be old Danny and do nothing or I could reinvent myself. Not by pretending to be someone I wasn't, but by actually *doing* something. I joined Rose, blocking Jefferson's line of sight to Toby.

'It's got in our heads, sir. It got in mine too. It's trying to drive us apart. We need to stick together and we can't do that without you. We need you, sir.'

Suddenly, Jefferson couldn't meet my gaze. He kept his eyes on the floor, but slowly lowered his gun.

Rose gave me a tiny nod of thanks, which, I confess, lit me up like a vodka shot. She ran to where Toby was crouched on the floor, eyes wide.

'You all right?'

'Yeah, um, dunno,' he whispered, his voice hoarse.

'Do you remember anything about that thing?'

He shook his head and hugged his knees.

'Try,' she told him, then ran to the communications console. 'Doctor, are you all right? Doctor?'

Zack came over the comms. 'We lost communication with the capsule when that thing severed the cable. I've still got life signs, but ... Rose, I'm sorry, there's no way back. They're stuck down there.'

'No,' she insisted. 'There's got to be a way. How much air do they have?'

I checked the instruments. 'An hour. Bit less.'

'We've got to get them back. We've got to.'

'Rose,' I said gently. 'They're ten miles down, we haven't got another ten miles of cable.'

She opened her mouth to reply, but she was cut off by a loud crack from the door to the drill room. The sound brought Jefferson back to himself. He put the safety back on his firearm and hurried to the door, pushing up the window cover. As he did, the Captain came over the comms:

'It's the Ood. They're cutting through the door-bolts, they're breaking in. Have you got the same?'

Jefferson looked through the window in the door as, outside, the Ood cut through another bolt. 'Yes, sir. Same on Door 25.'

Rose joined him, flinching as she saw the Ood pressed up against the glass. Its eyes flickered with a scarlet fire. 'How long's it gonna take?'

Jefferson grimaced. 'It's only a basic frame, should take . . . ten minutes, eight . . .'

Zack cut in from the command centre. 'I've got a security door, should last a bit longer, but that doesn't help you.'

Eight minutes until they were in here. I could almost smell burning flesh. My bravery in confronting Jefferson deserted me. I swallowed down anxiety as I looked around for somewhere we could hide.

Rose wasn't giving up. 'Right. So! We've got to stop them, or get out, or both.'

'I'll take both, yeah,' I said, hating how shrill my voice sounded. 'But how?'

'You heard the Doctor. Why d'you think that thing cut him off? Cos he was making sense, he was telling you to think your way out of this! Come on! For starters, we need some light. Zack, there's got to be some sort of power, somewhere?'

'Nothing I can do. Some captain! Stuck in here, pressing buttons.'

Rose wouldn't entertain his self-pity. 'But that's what the Doctor meant! Press the right buttons!'

'They've gutted the generators ...'

Rose heard the hesitation in his voice. 'What Zack? What?'

'The rocket's got an independent supply, if I can reroute that – Mr Jefferson! Open the bypass conduits, override the safety!'

Jefferson ran to the drill site command console and began work. 'Opening bypass conduits, sir!'

'Channelling rocket feed ...' Zack informed us, excitement building in his voice, '... now!'

There was a hum of engines and main power returned. The overhead lights flickered and then blasted the shadows from the room.

'That's it, there we go!' Rose yelled, delighted.

'Let there be light!' I shouted. Her enthusiasm was infectious.

For a few seconds, the comforting brightness made it feel as if everything had returned to normal, but then the overheads faded a little. The rocket's power was no match for the demands of the entire base. It was better than the gloomy emergency lighting, but not much.

'What about the Strategy Nine thing?' Rose asked, not wasting any time.

'Not enough power,' Jefferson said. 'We need it at a hundred percent.'

'Right, so we need a way out. Zack, Mr Jefferson, start working on that.' She turned her attention to Toby, who was getting to his feet. 'Toby, what about you?'

'I'm not a soldier, I can't do anything.'

'You're the archaeologist. What do you know about that Pit?'

He hugged his skinny frame and shook his head. 'Well, nothing. I can't even translate the language, but ...' He frowned, his voice trailing away. 'Hold on ... Maybe ...'

'What is it?'

'Since that thing was inside my head ... It's like, the letters make more sense to me ...'

'Then get to work, anything you can translate, just anything ...' She watched him sit at a monitor to start work, before turning her attention to me. 'As for you, Danny boy, you're in charge of the Ood. Is there anyway of stopping them?'

I shrugged. 'I don't know.'

She fixed me with her big brown eyes. 'Then find

out! Sooner we get control of the base, the sooner we can get the Doctor out!'

'If there's a way to do it, I'll find it.'

She grinned at me and planted a kiss on my forehead. 'Now get going! Shift!' She slapped me on the bum and headed over to join Jefferson. I was relieved that she didn't look back to see how much I was blushing or that I had to grab a clipboard to cover my, um, excitement.

Ida

As the dust settled in the cavern, we were able to assess the extent of the damage to the lift capsule. The impact of the falling cable had crushed its rectangular frame, which now leaned drunkenly. The console, which contained the comms unit, had been smashed to pieces. It wouldn't have made any difference if it had somehow miraculously survived; communications were dependent on the cable, which was now so much junk. The only part of the capsule to survive the disaster was the cable-drum. I looked at the cable, spooled over the cavern floor. Could we? There was only one way to try.

The Doctor frowned as I clambered over to get to the maintenance kit in the bottom of the capsule. There were cutters in there.

'We've got all this cable, might as well use it. Disconnect the drum, bring it down here. Feed the cable through the drum ...'

'And then what?' the Doctor asked, but his mouth was already curling into a smile at the absurdity of my idea.

'Abseil. Into the Pit.'

He laughed. 'Abseil! Right!'

I shrugged. 'We're running out of air, with no way back, it's the only thing we can do. Even if it's the last thing we ever achieve.'

'I'll get back. Rose is up there.'

The certainty in his voice filled me with a quiet confidence. He meant it. He was going to get back to his friend or die trying. I realised in that moment that I had become a different person in his company. Not only did his decency make me want to try for the impossible, but I could almost believe it was within my grasp. If you've never met him, then you couldn't understand the effect one person could have on you. What am I saying? You don't even believe he existed!

I didn't tell him how he changed me. I never had the chance. Instead, I told him to help me lug the cable-drum down to the rim of the Pit. He obliged, amused to play second-in-command to me for a little while. I think it was a novelty for him not to be in charge. He indulged me until I told him that I intended to be the one to abseil into the dark. 'I'm the senior officer. I go down.'

The Doctor was indignant. 'I'm no sort of officer, so I can do what I want.'

I told him it didn't work like that. It was my job.

'Only on paper,' he insisted. 'I've signed nothing, which gives me absolute freedom.'

I had to stop to rest. The weight of the drum felt as if it were pulling my arms from their sockets. The Doctor, naturally, seemed completely unaffected, merely waited patiently for me to get my breath back.

'We could always toss a coin, except I haven't got one. Well, I have, but . . .' He patted his environment suit. 'No way of reaching it.' He spun around with childish enthusiasm. 'I know! Let's try Scissors, Paper, Stone.'

'You're kidding?'

'D'you still do that? Scissors, Paper, Stone?'

'Yeah, but—'

'There we are then!' he interrupted. 'On the count of three.'

'Ready when you are,' I said, his enthusiasm gripping me.

We counted to three. I went for Paper, the Doctor made his fingers into Scissors.

'Scissors cut paper, I win. Thank you! I'm going down.'

'Best of three?'

The Doctor turned to me, suddenly serious. 'Ida, who has the best chance of saving us? Of saving Rose and everyone else up there?' He paused, but he wasn't waiting for an answer. He was right, of course. He was always right.

'Fair enough, I suppose,' I grumbled.

'And anyway, the game chose me. Don't mess with Scissors, Paper, Stone.'

We picked up the drum and carried on with our task.

'Mind you,' the Doctor added, with a grin, 'I should point out that I introduced the word "paper" into the conversation a couple of minutes back. Planted a suggestion. Which you subconsciously picked up. See how easy it is to put thoughts in someone's head?'

Creating a winch from the broken parts turned out to be harder than I imagined. The cable-drum was in full working order but finding a length of cable we could disentangle from the rest and cut free proved to be a more challenging task. The Doctor was all for leaping into the dark with the machinery untested, but I, the good scientist, insisted on testing our lash-up with a large rock first. Only when I was sure it would hold his weight did I fix the cable to a harness around the Doctor's environmental suit.

'That should hold it.'

The Doctor looked behind him, where the lip of the Pit gave way to ... nothing. 'Doesn't feel like such a good idea now.' Gingerly, he began to take small backward steps towards the drop. 'There it is again. That itch. Go down, go down, go down.'

Our eyes met; his were wide. Excitement? Trepidation? Or just plain fear?

'The urge to jump ...' I started, wanting to say something reassuring. 'D'you know where it comes from, that sensation? Genetic heritage, ever since we were primates in the trees. It's our bodies testing us, calculating whether or not we can reach the next branch.'

The Doctor almost let it go, but sometimes he couldn't resist letting me glimpse his superior understanding of ... well, everything. 'That's not it. That's too kind. Cos it's not the urge to jump, it's deeper than that. It's the urge to ... fall.'

And with that he took a step over the lip of the Pit and disappeared into the darkness.

The cable-drum spun wildly for a moment and I quickly activated the brake. For a second, I thought he might drop forever, but then the cable-drum slowed and finally stopped.

I stepped on the lip, careful where I placed my feet. 'Doctor,' I called down into the darkness. 'Are you okay?'

It only took a few seconds for the Doctor to reply, but my heart was in my mouth the whole time.

'Not bad, thanks. Wall of the Pit seems to be the same as the cavern, just ... not as much of it.'

The longer I peered down into the abyss, the more my eyes adjusted to the dark. I saw the glow of the Doctor's helmet torch, playing over the walls of the Pit. He was about twenty feet down.

'Seems to be a crust, sheers away to nothing a few feet below me. No cliff, nothing solid. Just darkness.'

'What do you want to do?' I asked.

'Lower me down.'

'Here we go then, nice and steady.'

The drum began to turn, spooling cable over the edge. I stood next to it, watching the light of the Doctor's helmet shrink until it became a faint glow, and then it was gone.

Interlude

Interlude

Extract from: INTERIM REPORT filed by KITZINGER, SANDRA. DETECTIVE. THIRD CLASS

All of the suspects claim that they were not in the company of the mysterious stranger known as 'the Doctor' when he descended into the pit. None of them could provide an account as to what took place below the surface of Krop Tor. All claim to have no idea how it led to the destruction of the Sanctuary 6 facility and, indeed, the entire planet.

As excuses go, it is absurdly childlike. The adult version of 'A big boy did it and runned away'. While I know the Sanctuary position is that this is a coordinated strategy cooked up between the suspects to evade responsibility, a couple of factors militate against this:

Firstly, their accounts all support each other's versions of events, but also contain glaring omissions, often to the detriment of their case. Most false alibis are too neat, too convenient. Their story is wildly implausible, yet their accounts consistently line up in terms of timeline and location.

Secondly, they behave like innocent people. It's a little-known fact that most serious offenders, particularly murderers, are relieved to be arrested, having been in a state of guilt-ridden anxiety for days if not weeks. For them, arrest is at least an end to uncertainty. Rather than protest their innocence, they often relax and are even known to fall asleep in their cells. Scott, Bartock and Cross Flane exhibit all the characteristics of the innocent.

My preliminary impression is that the three survivors believe what they are telling us. Of course, that is not to say it is the truth. Rather, given the impossibility of what they describe – the sudden arrival of advanced extraterrestrials, the unearthing of an ancient, religious evil – I suspect something happened between them, some traumatic event we have yet to understand, which led them to commit so wholeheartedly to these fantastical explanations.

Extract from: Sanctuary Corps response

While we are of course grateful for Detective Kitzinger's report, it is worth reiterating that she is employed as an investigator and not as a psychologist or psychiatrist. As such, her views on the mental capacity of the suspects should not be an influence on Sanctuary's commitment to prosecuting these suspects to the full extent of the law. Further, due to the sensitive nature of its contents, her report should remain within the protective confines of Sanctuary Corps' secret language.

Tilda Crow
VP Internal Affairs

Danny

I eat my lunch in the interrogation room, although lunch is too nice a description for a glass of water and a tray of Protein One. The food of prison inmates and explorers, basically because it's cheap and never goes off. Detective Kitzinger sits opposite me and smokes while I eat. I can't work out if that's an interrogation technique or just bad manners. I much prefer the other woman, who's better dressed and looks like she washes every day. However, she only sat in on my first interview before telling Detective Kitzinger that, 'I think I can leave this one to you,' and disappearing.

An Ood enters in a police officer's uniform, its translator globe hanging from a clip on its tunic. It hands Kitzinger a document for her signature. The memories it stirs make me tremble. *You will die here. This planet is your grave.* I have to take deep breaths to ward off a panic attack. I can't get used to the Ood being citizens. Their emancipation is one of the many changes that have taken place during our long sleep home. Kitzinger doesn't take her eyes off me whilst the Ood stands patiently waiting for her to finish with the document. When it reaches to take it from her, I can't help but flinch.

'I apologise for startling you,' it says, through its communicator.

Kitzinger runs her fingers through her cropped hair and smirks to herself. 'Mr Bartock, you really expect us to believe that the Ood turned on the crew and killed your friends?'

'I don't think it was the Ood, it was the thing that got inside them.'

'This –' she glances at her notes – 'Sartan.'

'Satan,' I correct her. 'It's an old Middle Eastern Earth name for adversary or accuser.'

She gives me a humourless smile as she takes a drag on her cigar. I glimpse her nicotine-stained teeth. 'You an expert now?'

'I've done some reading since I got back.'

'And this adversary, this –' she makes inverted commas with her fingers – '*devil* . . . it just took control of the Ood?'

'I've told you—'

'Constable,' she calls to the Ood that's preparing to leave. 'I'm a Detective with the Fifth Division, with a Class 3 Rating. Kill the prisoner. That's an order.'

The Ood blinks its creased, sore-looking eyes at its boss, but does not obey. 'I understand the point you are attempting to make, Detective Kitzinger, but at the risk of being insubordinate, I find it distasteful.'

Kitzinger turns and looks me in the eye. 'How about you explain how an Ood turns into a homicidal maniac?'

'I can't,' I say, holding her gaze. 'I can't explain how or why. I can only tell you how I stopped them.'

'*You* stopped them?'

'You don't have to sound so surprised.'

After I stood up to Jefferson, Rose and I became a team. I didn't have to go chasing after her attention any more; whenever I looked around, she was there, by my side.

'There's all sorts of viruses that could stop the Ood,' I told her, as I searched through their operation and care manual on the system. 'Trouble is, we haven't got them on board.'

She slapped the back of my chair. 'Well, that's handy, listing things we haven't got. We haven't got a swimming pool either, or a Tesco.'

'Look, I'm trying!' I said, wondering what the hell a Tesco was.

'Where do the Ood come from anyway?' She settled in the chair next to me, as I skimmed through background information on the Ood, searching for something, anything that might help.

'Way out in the Horsehead Nebula. They turned up at a colonists' outpost one day, asking to serve.'

Rose took that in. 'That doesn't make sense. How could a race evolve to serve? They'd get wiped out.'

'According to Ood Operations, they coevolved in a symbiotic relationship with other species.'

'Ood Operations?'

'The company that sells them.'

Rose looked incredulous. 'They're sold?! Maybe that thing down there isn't using the Ood – maybe it's *inspiring* them.'

I'd stopped paying attention to her Friends of the Ood rant. The answer was staring me in the face. A warning about the dangers of adverse feedback in the telepathic field.

Rose saw the expression on my face. 'What is it?'

'Oh my god, I can do it,' I said, turning to her, a smile breaking out on my face.

'Well, don't keep it to yourself.'

'The Ood are connected by the telepathic field, yeah? And we've got that monitor, testing the field, you saw it.'

'Yeah.' Rose frowned, already seeing the same challenges I was. 'Back in their room.'

'Yeah, I know, but if we do exactly what the manual tells us to avoid at all costs and *increase* feedback, it could disrupt their telepathy.'

'And?'

'Brainstorm! It'll tank them, spark out!'

'Can't you do it from here?'

'I've got to transmit it from the central monitor. We need to get to Ood Habitation.' I turned to the door where the Ood were slowly but surely breaking in. 'Through that door.'

Rose wasn't going to be put off. 'Okay, if that's what we have to do.' She ran over to Jefferson. 'Mr Jefferson, any way out?'

He was leaning over a table which he'd covered in hard copies of schematics of the base. He looked up, his face no longer haunted. He was a soldier with a problem to solve. 'There's a network of maintenance tunnels running underneath the base. We should be able to access it from here.'

Rose grinned. 'Ventilation shafts! You're talking about ventilation shafts.'

He gave her a wry smile. 'I appreciate the reference, but actually, that's not what they are. There's no ventilation down there. No air, in fact, none at all. They're built for machines, not life forms.'

Zack's voice chimed in from the command centre. 'I can manipulate the oxygen field from here, create discrete pockets of atmosphere. If I control it manually, I can follow you through the network.'

Rose looked between Jefferson and me. 'So ... we go down and you make the air follow us? By hand?'

'You wanted me pressing buttons,' Zack reminded her.

Rose exhaled. 'Yep, I asked for it.'

Zack chuckled over the comms. 'Don't worry. Manipulating force fields is what I do. How else do you think this crate holds together?'

'Right then,' Rose said, sounding more confident. 'We need to get to Ood Habitation, find a route for us.'

We worked quickly. It's not like we had a choice. Toby kept his eye on the door, warning us when the Ood were down to the final bolt. In moments, they'd be able to push the door out of its frame.

In the end, it was me who held us up. I wrote a simple program to remove the compressors from the telepathic field. Minute fluctuations in the field would be multiplied exponentially rather than be dampened. In a matter of seconds, the Ood's brains would short circuit. The problem was conforming the storage chip, which took agonising seconds.

'Danny! We don't have all day!' Jefferson hissed from the open access panel in the floor. 'They see us leave and they'll be straight after us.'

The monitor gave a happy chirrup as it completed the procedure. I ejected the storage chip and sprinted to join the others, who were ready to jump down through the access hatch.

'Feed this into the Ood Habitation monitor and it's a bad time to be an Ood!'

From the door, we heard the Ood snap the last bolt with their cutters.

Jefferson took charge. 'You go first, Danny, then you Miss Tyler, then Toby. I'll go last, in defensive position. Come on, quick as you can.'

As I dropped down into the maintenance tunnel, I heard Rose turn to Jefferson. 'We're coming back, you got that? We're coming back to this room and we're getting the Doctor out.'

She clambered down next to me and wrinkled her nose at the dank air. 'Is that you?' she whispered. 'You're not well.'

'Oh, laughing. Which way do we go?'

Zack's voice came over the comms. 'I'm here. Danny, just go straight ahead. I've got your life signs on my monitor. Keep going till I tell you otherwise.'

The maintenance tunnel was made of dark, metal panels, with rough edges where they had been screwed together. Dust had collected in the thin film of grease that coated the floor of the tunnel. My hands kept threatening to slide out from under me. The tunnel itself was only a few feet tall, so we had to scramble on all fours; Jefferson was right, it wasn't designed for people. Rose was behind me and Toby behind her.

'Not your best angle, Danny,' she teased.

'Stop it!' I told her, blushing.

'I dunno, could be worse,' Toby commented, from behind Rose.

'Oi!' Rose exclaimed indignantly.

Jefferson ordered us to be quiet as he replaced the airtight hatch. As he slotted it into place, we heard the door to the drill site clatter to the ground above us.

The Ood were in.

Zack

'If you want someone to blame for those who died that day, you can blame me. The lives of the crew were my responsibility. I failed them.'

The exec perks up when I tell them this. She joins her colleague at the table for the first time. Her smooth complexion tells me she's never put on an environmental suit, knows nothing of life off world. She appraises me with renewed interest.

'Are you saying you'd like to confess?'

'I didn't kill anyone, if that's what you mean. That thing at the bottom of the Pit did that. But it was my job to keep the crew safe. If anyone's culpable for the lives we lost, it's not Ida or Danny, it's me.'

The woman in the suit isn't impressed. She has narrow features, which her pinched expression only emphasises. Now she's sitting under the overhead light, I can see that she's older than I first thought. She may well be top-tier management at Sanctuary. If they sent the big guns, we really are in trouble.

Kitzinger, the detective, has been listening quietly. She reaches for a fresh cigar, but realises she's out. She winces to herself and distracts herself by fidgeting with her lighter. 'You said "that thing at the bottom of the Pit". You don't think it was the Devil?'

'I don't know what to call it, but that creature saw right into my soul and found me lacking. I'm not a gambling man, but if I had to put money on it, I'd bet I'll be seeing it again when I die.'

The woman in the suit leans in, doing her best to intimidate me. 'If you continue to insult our intelligence with your stories about doctors with magic boxes, you'll be reacquainting yourself with your devil sooner than you think.'

Kitzinger ignores her. 'What happened to the rest of the crew? Jefferson and Toby? I'm guessing not everyone escaped the Ood.'

I'd lied to Rose. I wasn't as confident about shaping pockets of air with force fields as I'd said. Sure, I'd used a field to stop the air escaping the breach when Scooti died, but that was a single force field blocking a doorway. Jefferson's plan to use the maintenance tunnels to get to Ood Habitation involved me operating multiple fields simultaneously. One miscalculation and they'd all asphyxiate.

I told myself that once Danny and the others were in the main shaft, they wouldn't be forced to move in single file; it'd be easier to keep them in an oxygenated bubble when they were moving two abreast. I filled my voice with as much confidence as I could muster. 'I'm feeding you air. Keep breathing. I've got you.'

I didn't take my eyes off the holographic representation of the labyrinth below decks. Danny, Toby and Jefferson were blinking blue lights, accompanied by their identity codes. There was an unidentified blue light between Danny and Toby, which had to be Rose.

My one thought was getting the team to Ood Habitation before the squidmouths at my door broke in. As the nerve centre of the base, the command centre was built to be secure. The Ood weren't going to find it as easy to break in here as they had the drill site, but I wasn't going to keep them out forever.

Danny reported that they'd made it to Junction 7.1. I watched the blinking lights huddle at a representation of the junction on the hologram in front of me. 'Okay, I've got you. I'm just aerating the next section.'

Staring at the task ahead, I realised I hadn't thought through the enormity of it. I was going to have to place one field on the other side of the bulkhead door, open the door and move two force fields simultaneously – one behind Jefferson and the others and one ahead of them.

Danny's voice came over the comms. 'Getting kinda cramped, sir, can't you hurry it up?'

I forced a light tone into my voice. 'Oi, bit of respect! I'm working on half power here.'

I heard Jefferson scold Danny. 'Stop complaining.'

'Mr Jefferson said, stop complaining,' Rose said, unnecessarily passing the instruction down the line. She'd forced a breeziness into her voice.

'I heard,' said Danny.

'He heard,' Rose reported back. That breeziness again. She was deliberately stopping anyone panicking. She was obviously no stranger to combat situations, although she didn't have a soldier's manner. Very little about the Doctor and his friend made sense.

Toby's voice sounded in my earpiece. He sounded nervous. 'Sir, the air's getting a bit thin.'

Rose piped up. '*He's* complaining now!'

'I heard!' Jefferson chimed in.

I had the fields in place. I was going to have to operate both the forward field and the bulkhead door with my left hand, whilst operating the rear force field with my right. The force-field controls were delicate: when I'd used them to stabilise the drill head, I'd operated a single field with both hands. There wasn't going to be any time to practise. What was I waiting for?

My fingers refused to move.

Rose made a joke about Danny farting. Poor kid sounded genuinely horrified to be accused by her. Could his crush be any more obvious?

'I'm just moving the air,' I lied. 'I've got to oxygenate the next section. Now, keep calm. The more air you use, the worse you're going to feel.'

Come on, come on, I told myself. *You can do this.*

I heard a faint, metal clang over the comms. Somewhere, a bulkhead door had opened. I brought up an internal security report and skimmed through the latest actions, whilst a chorus of concern came over the comms.

'What was that?' Danny asked, his voice shrill.

Rose was equally concerned. 'Mr Jefferson, what was that?'

'What was that noise?' Toby chimed in.

'Captain,' Jefferson asked, working hard to keep his voice steady. 'What was that?'

The news was bad. Why on earth did we think the Ood wouldn't be monitoring our communications?

'The junction in Habitation 5's been opened …

It must be the Ood. They're in the tunnels! They know where you are!'

Before I realised what I was doing, I'd activated the fields and opened the bulkhead.

Danny

I don't mind admitting that I was screaming for Zack to open the gate, when finally the bulkhead door slid up and I scuttled through. Rose followed, moving quickly on her hands and knees.

She activated her comms. 'Where are they, Zack? Are they close?'

The Captain's response was both instantaneous and measured. Nothing ever seemed to panic him. 'I can't tell, I can't see them. The computer doesn't recognise the Ood as proper life forms.'

'Well, whose idea was that!' Rose complained, as she ushered Toby through and waited for Jefferson to follow.

'Danny, turn left,' Zack ordered. 'Your immediate left.'

I didn't have to be told twice. I turned the corner and peered ahead into the darkness. Habitation 5 was behind us. We should have been safe for the moment, but it was possible the Ood had found other ways into the tunnels, ones that hadn't registered on the computer. Secondary tunnels intersected with the main one, little more than shadowy gaps in the dull metal walls. Who knew what could be waiting to spring out from them? I steeled myself and moved forward.

Behind me, Jefferson was asking Zack to keep the Ood off our backs. 'Can't you trap them? Cut off their air?'

'They're not relying on any,' Zack snapped back. His voice began to cut out as he spoke. 'Whatever's got ... hold ... them ... away their need for it ...'

'Sir! Are you there?' I started. If we lost contact with Zack, we'd be running blind and at the mercy of the Ood.

'I'm here. The Ood are using acetylene torches on the command centre door. They're almost in.' Despite the danger he was in, he remained utterly focused on saving us. 'Danny, turn right, go right, faster.'

I turned into one of the smaller tunnels. It was pitch black. 'Are you sure, sir?'

'Just do as you're told. They're gaining on you.'

We made it to the next bulkhead together, waited agonising seconds for Zack to manipulate the fields, then the bulkhead door engaged rarely used gears as it lifted up and we were scrambling through. We made it through three bulkheads like this, the metal floor of the maintenance tunnels cold beneath our hands and knees; a reminder that the atmosphere was personal and temporary.

At the fourth bulkhead we heard a chilling sound from the direction we'd come. Scuttling feet.

The Ood had found us.

Rose hauled Toby through the bulkhead doorway and then reached for Jefferson, who shook his head. 'I'll maintain a defensive position.'

'You can't stop here!'

Jefferson checked the ammunition in his gun. 'Miss Tyler, that's my job. You've got your task, now see to it.'

Crouched at the junction, Rose looked like she wasn't going anywhere without him.

'Miss Tyler, go now, that's an order. I'll follow.'

There was the pattering of Ood feet from further down the corridor. Toby glanced back wide-eyed and ushered Rose to move. 'You heard what he said, shift!'

Reluctantly, Rose moved past me on her hands and knees, Toby crawling anxiously after her.

Jefferson raised his gun to his eye so he could look down the sights. He was sweating but determined. He caught me staring. 'Go, Danny,' he hissed.

I nodded and chased the others down the narrow tunnel. As I caught up with Rose and Toby, I heard gunfire from behind me. I glanced back: the tunnel was strobing with the light from automatic fire. An Ood was shredded by bullets. Jefferson had his back to the junction wall, his boots braced against either side of the entrance to the smaller tunnel, his face set as he fired in short, controlled bursts at the oncoming Ood.

It was the last time I ever saw him.

Zack

Jefferson hanging back meant that I had to set up two new fields to cradle the air around him. The power in the station was so low that the fields themselves were barely strong enough to contain the atmosphere around the crew; they'd be no barrier to the Ood. I urged Jefferson to follow the others, but all I got back over the comms was the sharp clatter of gunfire.

Cold sweat slid down my back. I couldn't keep both pockets of air operational for long. 'Jefferson, did you copy? You have to move!'

When a reply came, it wasn't Jefferson.

'Open 8.2!' Danny yelled. 'Open 8.2! Zack! Can you hear me? Open 8.2!'

'Clear the line, Danny, I need to speak to Jefferson.'

'Open it now!'

Infuriated by his self-centredness, I quickly operated the bulkhead door.

'Come on, Zack!' Danny was almost screaming.

'I'm trying!'

Something was wrong. The bulkhead door should have opened. A small alert was chiming on my console, one note in a symphony of alarms. I saw the problem. Bulkhead Door 8.2 connected to the main passage; it wouldn't open without the previous door closing.

'Jefferson?'

Danny's voice cut in. 'We have incoming Ood!'

'What? How far?'

'We can hear them coming!'

'Get off the comms.'

'What? No!'

'Jefferson's on your channel. I need him to move!'

The line cleared. 'Jefferson! Did you hear that?'

'Loud and clear. I'm on my feet. Well, knees.'

'Get past 8.1. ASAP!'

The flashing blue light that was Jefferson began to move along the corridor.

I moved Danny on to a different channel. 'How much time until the Ood are on you?'

'Open the door now!'

'Danny. How many seconds till they're there?'

'I dunno! Twenty?'

'Exactly, Danny! How many exactly? Jefferson's life depends on it!'

Rose's voice cut in. 'Twenty-five. And we need five to get through once it's up.'

'Thanks, Rose,' I switched channel. 'Jefferson—'

'I heard,' he cut me off. He was panting hard. I could hear his hands and knees thundering on the metal floor as he raced along the passage.

I watched his progress on the hologram of the base. With the little finger and thumb of one hand, I moved the two fields containing Jefferson's air pocket, while preparing to close 8.1 with my index finger. With my right hand I prepared to open 8.2 to save Rose, Danny and Toby. I counted down the last few seconds out loud. Sweat dripped from my fingers onto the controls. My right hand was so tense, I feared it might spasm.

I watched Jefferson's blue flashing light approaching 8.1.

'Three. Two. Move it, Jefferson!'

He wasn't going to make it.

'I'm there! I'm there!' Jefferson yelled. 'Close the door.'

I brought 8.1 down and immediately opened 8.2, sliding their respective air pockets across the thresholds.

'Danny? Toby? Did you make it? Report!'

Danny's voice came over the comms. For an awful moment, I thought his shrieks were pain, but he was laughing, hysterically, with relief. 'We made it, sir! We made it!'

Relief flooded through me. I'd done it. I kept my promise. No one had died on my watch. 'Jefferson, rejoin the others.'

There was a pause. I heard him let out a sigh.

'Jefferson?'

When he spoke, his voice was barely more than a whisper. 'Regret to inform you, sir. I was a little slow. Not so fast, these days.'

Cold stone landed in my guts. 'What are you talking about? You said . . .'

'A white lie. I hope you'll forgive me. I wasn't going to let my inertia cause my fellows to fall.'

I slammed my hands on the control to open 8.1, but it wouldn't open now the air was gone from the next section. 'I can't open the bulkhead now! Jefferson, what have you done?'

'I hope I've bought them a little time, sir.'

'Don't you understand? There's nothing I can do!'

I heard him exhale and slump to the ground. 'You've done enough, sir. Made a very good captain, under the circumstances. Might I ask that you deactivate the force fields and speed up the removal of the oxygen in this section?'

Over the comms, I could hear the sounds of scurrying footsteps. They were getting louder. Incoming Ood.

'John?'

'The enemy is upon me. Lack of air seems a preferable departure, than ... well, let's say, death by Ood.' He chuckled, softly. 'I would appreciate it, sir.'

And when it came to it – the moment I'd dreaded for so long – the right words came without being searched for. 'God speed, Mr Jefferson.'

'Thank you, sir.'

I lifted my thumb from the control pad. Heard a faint release of air over the comms.

The blue flashing light that was Jefferson winked off.

I took a long, slow breath. 'Report: Officer John Maynard Jefferson, P.K.D.,' I told the log. 'Deceased, with honours, Forty-three K, Two Point One.'

Danny

We'd all heard Mr Jefferson's last words over the comms. All of us staring back the way we'd come, willing him to appear out of the dark.

After a few moments, I called the Captain: 'Zack, we're at the final bulkhead, 9.2. And, uh, if my respects could be on record. Mr Jefferson saved our lives.'

When the Captain spoke, there was a new maturity in his voice. 'Noted. Opening 9.2.'

As I turned to lead the way, I saw an Ood's regulation boots appear behind the rising door. I pushed Rose behind me, just as the Ood's deadly communication globe filled the passageway with white light.

Rose beat me to the comms. 'Lower 9.2! Zack, lower it!'

I winced as the bright little translator globe darted towards me like a viper. The bulkhead door slammed down with such force it sliced through the cable that connected the Ood's deadly globe to its body. The globe's light died suddenly, and I heard rather than saw it bounce on the floor and roll away in the dark.

As my eyes readjusted to the gloom, Toby started to panic. 'We can't go back, 8.2's sealed off. We're stuck!'

Rose ignored him, looking around for another way out. 'If we can't go back, we'll go up. Up there. Look.'

I hadn't seen the panel in the ceiling. Rose braced her back against it and rammed her elbow into it. With a couple of shoves, she'd forced the panel open. The overhead lights from the corridor above us felt as bright as sunlight. I blinked away their glare and clambered up after her. We turned back to haul Toby out, but he wasn't there.

'Toby, get out of there!' Rose yelled.

He appeared from the darkness. 'Help me, oh my god, they're coming.'

Rose and I grabbed an arm each and hauled him out. I tried to shut the panel after us, but it was too bent out of shape. I abandoned it and headed down the corridor, pulling Rose after me. 'We can get to Ood Habitation this way.'

I raced to the end of the corridor and ordered the computer to open the door.

'Door 38 open.'

I waited ten seconds for the computer to release the magnetic lock on the door, then quickly spun the wheel to open it. Rose grabbed the wheel to help. As the environmental seal broke, we immediately heard the clang of footfalls on the metal walkway on the other side of the door. We were already pushing the door closed, when we saw the squidmouths marching towards us.

'What now?' Rose demanded, pressing herself against the door, until the computer informed us that it was safely locked.

I needed to think. The Ood were in Section 1. That wasn't good. The base was made of six sections; we knew the Ood at the drill site in Section 3 were possessed, but if the Ood in Section 1 had gone bad too, then the chances were they all had. Given that each of the six sections housed a dozen Ood, our options were going to shrink very quickly.

And then I realised that the problem might contain the solution.

'This way. Come on.'

I led Rose and Toby back the way we'd come. If the Ood in all the sections were possessed, that meant they were all connected. I didn't need to get to Habitation 3, I could use any of the habitations.

We made our way to Section 2 without encountering any Ood. As I opened Habitation 2, Zack's voice came over the comms:

'Hurry it up! They're through!'

There were six Ood in the pen. As soon as they registered our movement, they rose calmly to their feet and turned to look up at us, their eyes burning red.

'Get it in, transmit!' Rose yelled, looking around for something to fend off the Ood, who were already moving to the stairs.

For a moment, I couldn't get the chip into the port. Had I messed up? Used the wrong-sized chip? The adrenalin coursing through my body was so intense that it took me seconds to realise that there was another storage chip already in the port. I tugged it out and sent it skittering across the floor.

'Danny!' Rose yelled.

The squidmouths had reached the top of the stairs. The nearest lifted its communication globe out of its pocket and it began to glow in its gloved hand. The globe lifted into the air and reared back to strike like it was alive. I slammed the chip into the port.

Nothing happened.

Zack

When I faced my death, I was calm.

I don't know if witnessing Jefferson's grace made it easier to experience my own. Perhaps it put my life in perspective? Did I really think I was so special that I should survive when others had fallen?

The Ood had cut a perfect rectangular line within the frame of the door. Even in mutiny, they were methodical. They forced the door from the other side, and the slab of reinforced steel hit the floor of the command centre, with an almighty clang that left my ears singing like a soprano.

'*Broken Door 1,*' the computer informed me uselessly.

The Ood stepped through the smoking doorway in single file, spreading out to make a line, their communication globes glowing brightly in their palms. As they marched towards me, I ordered them to stand down. Like that was ever going to happen. My voice was hoarse with thick fumes from the door. They ignored me. I shouted all the deactivation commands I could think of, but still they came for me, their eyes burning with scarlet fire.

I raised the bolt gun and took aim. There was one bolt in the chamber. I fired point blank at the nearest Ood. The bolt travelled too fast for me to see it enter its pale flaky forehead, which seemed to explode from within. The Ood took a step forward, and for a second I thought it was going to defy death – but it stumbled and toppled over onto its side.

'Take another step and you'll get the same,' I lied.

The next Ood stepped over its fallen comrade and held out its glowing sphere to me, like a ghastly present. I don't know if it knew that I was out of ammunition or just didn't care. The globe lifted from its palm and hovered, ready to lash out.

I waited for the end, but it didn't come. Instead, the Ood all started to scream. Not through their communicators – from their throats. It was the first time I ever heard them make a noise that wasn't artificially created. It was shrill and painful to hear in more ways than one. They clutched their heads and stumbled around the command centre, before crashing to the ground, inert.

Danny had pulled it off. Over the comms, I heard Rose, Danny and Toby whooping with delight.

'Zack, we did it!' Rose yelled. 'The Ood are down!'

I heaved out a long breath. 'Bit scary there for a moment.'

Danny came on: 'Yeah, the feedback took a little longer to build than I thought.'

'But in the circumstances,' I said, and felt a smile curl at the corner of my mouth, 'not bad.'

'Thanks, Captain.'

Rose's voice replaced his. 'Now we have to get the Doctor.'

The Doctor and Ida. I stepped over the Ood bodies and made my way to the door. As I did, I slipped on something hard, which rolled out from under my foot. It was the bolt cylinder from the gun; designed to put a hole through steel, it had passed through the Ood's skull without a scratch.

I slipped it back into the chamber of the gun, thinking it might come in handy, and stowed it in my belt.

That small bolt of steel would save the universe.

Ida

I don't know how far the Doctor descended into the Pit. There was no way of measuring the stretch of cable we were able to free from the ten miles of it that fell from the bottom of the borehole. Did I let out a single mile or five? We had no idea how deep the Pit was, or what the Doctor would find at the bottom.

He didn't stop talking as I winched him down into the unknown, chatting away to me over the suit comms, as if we were sitting in a bar, chewing the fat over drinks.

'You get representations of the horned beast, right across the universe,' he said. 'The myths and legends of a million worlds. Earth. Draconia. Vel Consadine, Daemos, the Kaled God of War ... The same image, over and over again ... Maybe that idea came from somewhere. Bleeding through. A thought at the back of every sentient mind.'

There was hardly any cable left in the drum. What would happen if it ran out – when it ran out?

'Emanating from here?' I asked, distracting myself.

'Could be.'

'If this is the original ... does that make it real, does that make it the actual Devil, though?'

'If that's what you want to believe. Maybe that's what the Devil is, in the end. An idea.'

I watched the last of the cable leave the drum, exposing the large, heavy-duty clamp. It came to a stop. The metal cable thrummed with tension as it stretched across the floor of the cavern, before disappearing down into the Pit. The Doctor was so far down now and still hadn't touched the bottom.

'That's it. That's all we've got.'

For a moment, he didn't say anything. I could only imagine what was going through his mind, as he hung there in the void.

'You getting any kind of readout?' I asked tentatively.

'Nothing. Could be miles to go. Or, could be thirty feet. There's no way of telling.' He paused for a moment. 'I could survive thirty feet.'

'Oh no you don't, I'm pulling you back up.' I hit the control to throw the drum into reverse.

The irritating buzzing of his sonic device came over the comms. The cable-drum stopped. I stabbed the controls, but he'd disabled them with his casual genius.

'You bring me back, we're just gonna sit there and run out of air. I've *got* to go down.'

'You can't. Doctor, you can't.'

I don't know what I was more frightened of, him falling to his death, or me slowly asphyxiating alone.

'Call it an act of faith.'

'I don't want to die on my own.'

'I know,' he said, gently.

I heard a click of what I feared was his harness.

'Doctor?'

But his voice came back over the suit comms, quiet in my ear. 'Never did ask. Have you got any sort of faith?'

'Not really. Brought up Neo Classic Congregational. That's cos of my dad, he was ...' It was suddenly hard to swallow. 'Oh, my poor dad.'

'That creature said you were running from him. Do you want to talk about it?'

And I was back at Dad's bedside, his hands clawing at me, and then running down the white hospital corridors, to get anywhere, to get away, to put as much distance between us as I could.

Well, I told myself, *you really succeeded in that, didn't you.*

'Neo Classics, have they got a devil?' the Doctor asked, changing the subject.

I tried to brighten my tone; I'm not sure that I succeeded. 'No, not as such. Just ... the things that men do.'

And women, I thought.

'Same thing, in the end.'

'Yeah ... What about you?'

The Doctor exhaled sharply, a crackle in my ear. 'I believe ...' he started, and then paused, as if no one had asked him this before. 'I believe I haven't seen everything. I dunno. Funny, isn't it? The things you make up. The rules. If that thing had said it came from beyond the universe, I'd believe it, but *before* the universe? Impossible. Doesn't fit my rules. Still. Maybe that's why I keep travelling. To be proved wrong.' He paused and added. 'Thank you, Ida.'

And I knew, in that moment, that he was going to undo the last clasp.

'Don't go,' I pleaded, surprised by how like a child I sounded.

'If they get back in touch ... If you talk to Rose, just tell her ... tell her ...'

He sounded both terrified and serene, all at the same time.

'Oh, she knows,' he murmured.

I heard the metallic click of the last clasp being released.

Zack

The only Ood I came across on my journey across the base were inert. I found Rose, Danny and Toby at the drill site. Rose was hunched over the control console, yelling into the comms mic.

'Doctor, can you hear me? Ida? Doctor? Are you there?'

I was so relieved to see them alive. I'd been alone in the command centre for what felt like days. I resisted an urge to hug them, but only just.

'The comms are still down,' I said. 'But I think I can patch them through the central desk and boost the signal.'

Rose raced over and threw her arms around me. 'Thank you, thank you, thank you.'

'Just give me a minute.'

After manipulating complex force fields simultaneously for an hour, rerouting communications via the ship to the drill site was straightforward, even when your hands were shaking as much as mine. Rose stood next to me, watching me work with mounting anticipation at being reunited with her friend.

'You saved us. We would've died down there without you.'

I looked over to where Danny was standing with Toby. Danny's hands and knees were covered in grime from the tunnels, but there was a new confidence about him. He'd come into himself down there in the dark. 'That was Danny,' I said, both about him and to him. 'He saved us all.'

Danny had the good grace to look abashed at my compliment. 'Teamwork,' he said.

I nodded and turned to Rose. 'Okay, we're up and running. Be my guest.'

Rose grabbed the microphone and activated the comms system. 'Doctor? Doctor?'

Nothing.

She turned to me. 'I don't think it's working.'

'Give it a chance.'

'Are you there? Doctor?'

There was a long pause where no one said anything. In our desperate bid to save our own lives, there hadn't been time to think of Ida and the Doctor's fate. Finally, the channel came alive, but it wasn't the Doctor who spoke, it was Ida.

'He's gone.' She sounded detached. I wondered if she was in shock.

Rose frowned, incredulous. 'What do you mean, gone? Gone where?'

'He fell. Into the Pit. Don't know how deep it is. Miles and miles and miles.'

'But ... what d'you mean, he fell?'

'I couldn't stop him.' I heard her stifle a sob. 'He said your name.'

Rose stood there, frozen, holding the comms mic out in front of her. Two shellshocked people hanging on either end of a line. I stepped forward and gently took the mic from her hands.

'I'm so sorry, Rose,' I whispered and then stepped away to speak to Ida. 'It's Zack. There's no way of reaching you. No cable, no back-up, you're ten miles down, we can't get there.'

'You should see this place, Zack. It's so beautiful. I wanted to discover things, and here I am.' Her voice echoed in a place I would never get to see, and which she could never leave.

'Ida, we've got to abandon the base. I'm declaring the mission unsafe. All we can do is make sure no one ever comes here again.'

'We'll never find out what it was.'

I thought about Jefferson. 'Maybe that's for the best.'

'. . . Yeah.'

I couldn't let it end like that. I tried to think of something formal to say. 'Officer Scott,' I started, but she cut me off.

'It's all right. Just go. Good luck.'

'And you.' I put the comms mic down and felt a wave of sadness that threatened to overwhelm me. But I couldn't cave; I knew we weren't out of this yet. I took a breath to keep the emotion at bay and turned to Danny and Toby. 'Close down the feed-links, get the retrotopes online. Then get to the rocket and strap yourselves in. We're leaving.'

I moved off, already thinking of the hundred tasks that needed to be completed to safely shut down the base before we left. That was when Rose told me that she wasn't coming with us. She was calm, matter-of-fact, but resolute.

I turned back. 'Rose, we've got room for you.'

She dug her hands into the pockets of her jeans. 'I'm gonna wait for the Doctor. Just like he'd wait for me.'

'I'm sorry, but he's dead.' I saw Danny flinch at my straight talking, but sugar-coating the truth wasn't going to help Rose. She was lost in grief. They say there's five stages of it. I don't remember them all, but the big one is definitely denial.

'You don't know the Doctor,' she insisted, her voice cracking. 'Cos he's not. I'm telling you, he's not. And even if he is. How can I leave him? All on his own. All the way down there. I've got to stay.'

I looked over to Danny and Toby, who were staring at me, waiting to see what I was going to do. I gave them a little nod, which I hoped they'd understand, then I turned back to Rose, who was staring down into the depths of the borehole.

'Then... I apologise for this. Danny, Toby, make her secure.'

They hurried over to her, pulling her away from the borehole. She didn't realise what was happening at first. When it dawned on her, she started to struggle.

'No! Let go of me! I'm not going!'

The more she fought, the more determined Danny and Toby became. As she realised she was losing the battle, she became feral, kicking at them.

'Let go of me! I said – let go of me!'

'I've lost too many people,' I said, although she couldn't hear me for screaming. 'I'm not leaving anyone else behind.'

There was a medical kit on the wall. I took an anaesthetic pen that could floor a Judoon, pressed it against her neck and hit the activation stub. She shouted, looking so angry, so betrayed. Then she slumped into unconsciousness.

'Let's get her on board.'

I put Rose over my shoulder and headed out of the drill site. I tore up evacuation protocols that were vying for space on a list in my head, and told the others to get to the ship. We were leaving immediately.

The gantry that led to the rocket silo was littered with the bodies of the Ood. Rose started to slide off my shoulder as I stepped over them and, as I paused to heave her back up, I noticed that several of the Ood were moving. Not much. Little flexes of their hands, jerks of their heads, leaving their fronds quivering.

'Danny,' I said, nodding towards the movement.

'It's the telepathic field, it's reasserting itself.'

I asked him how long we had, but he only shrugged. I redoubled my pace and urged everyone to get to the rocket.

I laid Rose on an acceleration couch, fastened her safety belt and then paused to get my breath back. The cockpit of the rocket smelt musty. Only the dim overhead lights were on, having automatically activated when we entered. There was a thin film of dust on the pilot's chair. I doubted anyone had been here since we made planetfall eight months ago. I had piloted the craft down onto the planet after the Captain died. What should have been a celebratory moment had felt more like a funeral. And this was hardly a triumphant return.

I slid into the Captain's chair and ran through the preflight procedures. Despite having drawn power from the ship to keep the base running these last few hours, there was still more than enough to escape the pull of the planet – assuming the gravity funnel remained operational.

As Toby and Danny took their places behind me, I realised that that the mission, cursed pretty much from the start, had failed absolutely. We still had no idea who or what had created the gravity funnel and we were no closer to understanding the source of its power, or what enabled the planet to resist the greatest force in the universe. All we had learnt was that the cosmos was infinitely more terrifying than our worst nightmares. I vowed if I made it home, I would never venture into space again.

The power plant reached operational mass; I felt the rocket tremble beneath me. The manoeuvre drive indicated its readiness to receive power. Once we made it to the edge of the system, I could plot the jump home.

I looked out of the horizontal slot of the cockpit window. The rocky surface of the planet was barely visible through the darkened glass. 'Say goodbye, guys.'

I connected the power feed and felt the pressure of the manoeuvre drive start to build. 'Dislocating

B clamp, C clamp, raising blu-nitro to maximum. Toby, how's the negapact feed-line?'

'Clear, ready to go, sir,' he said. 'Oh, for god's sake, get us out.'

Danny leant forward and indicated Rose, who was starting to stir. 'Captain, I think we're gonna get a problem passenger.'

'Keep an eye on her,' I said, twisting back in my seat to prepare for lift-off. I'd hoped we'd be off world before she realised what I'd done.

'What did you . . . ?' Rose started, looking around wildly. 'Where's . . . but we're not . . .'

I kept my eyes forward, but heard Danny say, 'It's all right, Rose, we're safe, we're going, we're leaving.'

First came confusion. 'But I didn't . . .' Then anger. 'I'm not going anywhere! Get me out of this thing! Let me out!'

I didn't look back; I couldn't meet her gaze. Instead, I kept my eyes focused on the horizon and, without bothering to count down, I activated the drives.

'Lift-off.'

The manoeuvre drive slammed me back in my chair. I was born in the gravity well of a planet, but had lived most of my life in space. My body had acclimatised to this kind of acceleration long ago. Despite her distress, Rose had fallen silent. Either the pressure on her larynx was leaving her unable to speak, or the g-force had knocked her out. I hoped she wasn't in pain.

We exchanged the acceleration force of take-off for the turbulence of the gravitational funnel. The old rocket rattled and shook, and at times felt like it was going to tear itself apart, but we were no longer in danger of our organs being punctured by the acceleration. The instant Rose felt it lose its grip, she was fighting with her safety belt.

'I'm not leaving him! I'm not! I'm never going to leave him!'

Before anyone could stop her, she'd shrugged off her safety harness, leant forward and grabbed the bolt gun from my belt. It happened so quickly that she'd slipped off the safety catch and pressed it against the back of my head before I'd been able to react.

'Take me back to the planet. Take me back!'

Slowly, I turned round to face her. The bolt gun was trembling in her hand.

'Or what?' I said, as softly as I could.

'Or I'll shoot.'

A solitary tear ran down her cheek. She brushed it away with the back of her free hand. All her strength, all the bravado she'd shown to keep everyone together, was gone. Standing there, shaking, desperately not wanting to face the truth, she looked so young. It occurred to me in that moment that she was barely in her twenties, perhaps no more than a teenager.

'Would you, though?' I asked. 'Would you really? Is that what your Doctor would want?'

For a long moment, we faced each other. Me looking down the barrel of a gun, hoping that Rose really was the person she'd seemed to be over the last few hours.

She faltered, and lowered her makeshift weapon.

'I'm sorry, Rose. But it's too late, anyway. I can't turn the ship back.' I indicated for her to look out of the starboard porthole. 'Take a look.'

She did as I asked, leaning her head against the thick glass of the window. I didn't have to look to know what she would see. The planet receding below us, and with it, the Doctor, or what remained of him.

'This is what the Doctor would have wanted for you. He'd want you to live, yeah?'

She pressed her forehead against the glass as if she might break it, and with it the truth that she couldn't bear to face.

Somebody giggled. It was Toby. It was so inappropriate, so thoughtless, I wanted to smack him.

Danny was similarly outraged. 'What's the joke?'

'Just . . . we made it!' Toby was grinning broadly, completely oblivious to Rose's pain. 'We escaped! We actually did it!'

Rose clambered back across the cramped cockpit to her seat. 'Not all of us,' she said, without looking at Toby. She strapped herself back into her safety harness.

'We're not out of it yet,' I said. 'We're just the first people in history to fly *away* from a black hole. Toby, give me an update.'

Toby checked the screen on the panel above his head. 'Stats at 53, funnel stable at 66.5, hull pressure constant. Smooth as we can, sir, all the way home.'

He looked me right in the eye and giggled again. I remember thinking that there was something really wrong with that boy. He shook his head at some private joke and returned his attention to his work.

'Preparing to make the jump to Earth.'

Ida

I felt a vibration through my body as I sat at the edge of the Pit. The rocket leaving. I can't explain how I knew the tremors came from above and not below, but I felt with a great certainty that it was the others escaping this godforsaken place.

I wish I could tell you I was filled with joy that they had made it, but the truth is, all I felt was sadness for myself; a selfish fear of – if not death itself – then the agony and terror that must surely accompany it. I watched the oxygen monitor on my suit sink slowly but steadily into the red. I considered launching myself into the Pit and joining the Doctor in its depths – at least that would have been quick – but I'm a coward by nature and remained frozen where I sat.

The truth is I missed the Doctor. Missed is too small a word. You spend time in his company, feel the sunlight warmth of his attention, and, when it's removed, the world feels colder, less certain, more threatening. His brilliance is like a force field that protects him from the dangers of life and, in his company, you can't help but feel that protection extends to you. When he leaves you, you realise that you've been left with nothing but the air in your lungs, and there'll be nothing left to breathe in once you exhale.

I felt a sudden flare of rage that the Doctor had abandoned me, followed by an urgent desire to remove my helmet. I was fumbling with the clasps, when the insanity of what I was trying to do registered in my conscious mind. It was the first symptom of asphyxiation. I couldn't get a breath and my monkey brain was telling me the cause was the glass bowl on my head and the solution was to take it off.

My visor steamed up with panic. There was no more air in the suit, nothing to suck down into my lungs. For a few seconds, I sat in the moment between my last breath and its consequences.

Oh god, please don't let it hurt.

I became aware of the surface of my lungs; grew acquainted with every capillary demanding oxygen and their burning fury when they were denied. My ears filled with the bump of my heartbeat, I felt the pulse on my forehead throb, as if it were a parasite trying to fight its way out of my skin.

It was too soon. I didn't want to die. There was so much I wanted to do. Not the big stuff, the missions to the stars. I was done with ambition and success and glory. I wanted more Sundays, more pizza, more sandwiches, more drinks with friends. Oh god, I wanted to have put it right with Dad.

And then there was only pain. An agony in my head that chased all the words and thoughts away. A thousand migraines thumping in my skull, until my vision narrowing and the world receding was a welcome sign of the end.

I finish telling my story and sit back in my chair. You stare at me for a few moments, then reach for one of your cheap cigars and tap it on the table before lighting it, much to your colleague's irritation.

'And then what?' Your voice, husky with smoke.

'I woke up on the ship, strapped into an acceleration couch.'

'And how did you get there?'

'I have no idea.'

Next to you, the suited exec shakes her head in irritation. 'Do you seriously expect us to believe that?'

You scratch your salt and pepper crewcut. 'As a lie, it's hardly compelling,' you reply without looking at her.

'Look,' I tell you. 'You've interviewed Danny and Zack. You must know what happened to the base. They said—'

'I'm not interested in whatever story you cooked up with your friends on the way home,' the exec snaps. 'I need the truth.'

'That's what you got. I'm sorry it's inconvenient for your bottom line.'

The Sanctuary exec leaves, already typing a report into her device on her way out. You and I are alone for the first time since I've been detained. You gather up your pack of cigars and your lighter, and stuff them into one of the sagging pockets of your overcoat. As you're about to get up, you hesitate.

'They're gonna offer you a plea tomorrow. It won't be a great one, but you should take it.'

'Are they paying you to tell me to take it?'

You shrug, not offended by my accusation. 'I'm not in their pocket. I'm on the police service dime. But you're right to be wary. I'm just here so the company can say the investigation was independent and they ticked all the boxes.'

'I'm glad to see my taxes are well spent.'

'I've been a cop a long time. I don't know if you're telling the truth, but I do know that you *think* you are. Something bad happened back on that planet and this is the only way your mind can deal with it. With devils and heroes and magic boxes.'

'The Doctor was real.'

'You're never gonna convince an adjudicator of that. And Sanctuary are going to throw the book at you. They need a conviction because if it's negligence then that whole base is an insurance claim for them. This story of yours is the worst possible tale you could tell – you've made what happened to their precious base an Act of God. Or an act of the other guy. Either way, they won't recoup their loss.'

'You're saying I should lie?'

'I'm saying you can't win with the truth. Or whatever you believe the truth to be.'

The following morning, the exec turns up with an offer, just as you said she would. If I admit that I wilfully destroyed the base, they will ask for life imprisonment at an off-world penal colony, but if I insist on pleading not guilty, they will ask for the death penalty if I'm found culpable for the murders of Jefferson, Scooti, Toby and the others. I tell her that I need to think about it, and she seems to accept that. Anything but an immediate refusal has to be a positive for her. I have until the court date to give her my answer.

The week until court drags by. I don't see anyone except an Ood who works for a prisoners' visiting service. It's hard to get used to the transformation of the Ood that has taken place whilst we slept. Their liberation is as beautiful as their lobotomised captivity was monstrous. Mostly it sits quietly and listens as I try to weigh up the decision I must make. It says little about itself. When I ask its name, it tells me that it would be too hard for me to pronounce and its globe cannot translate it. Its old designation is still printed on the breast pocket of its jacket. Delta 4 Delta. I call it Deedee and it doesn't seem to mind. Sometimes it sings quietly when I have nothing to say. I'd forgotten they sing – simple, ethereal melodies that rise and fall, often with breaks as if they are listening to a response only they can hear. I asked Deedee why it hasn't returned to its homeworld with the majority of its kind. It told me that it still has a debt to pay to the man who liberated them but wouldn't say more.

On the day my case is being heard, I'm permitted to shower and presented with a simple, grey suit to wear in court. My hands are cuffed before I'm led out of the interrogation building to a waiting prisoner transport, which has high sides and small tinted windows placed near the roof. As I'm driven through the city, I spy the rooftops of buildings, tall trees and a few blimps pulling advertising banners across the sky. Whatever I say in court, whether my future is death or exile, this will be my last glimpse of home.

As we slow outside the court building, I hear chanting. I can't make out the words, I wonder if there is a big trial taking place in another courtroom. It's only when the back door to the transport is opened and people begin to scream, that I realise the crowds have been waiting for me. I step down from the vehicle, blinking in the sudden brightness of the day. For a moment, I'm touched, thinking these people believe I'm innocent and are here to support me. But I see the placards they're carrying have images of horned devils. Other placards bear slogans like *The End is Nigh*, *Repent Now* and *Abaddon Comes!*

I have attracted religious zealots. They have come neither to support nor condemn me, but to revel in the fervour of the apocalypse.

They scream at me. Their eyes wide with anticipation, their mouths glistening and wet with excitement. It's impossible to pick out individual voices. I turn away and hide my face from them. What do they want from me? Do they think I'm

Hell's emissary come to make them burn? Or do they think I can offer them some form of absolution? I hurry into the courthouse, all but dragging my prison escort behind me.

The building is cool and quiet as I stand panting for breath. The corridors are high with flagged stone floors and marble walls. Statues of long-dead adjudicators line the corridors. I'm met by the counsel that has been appointed to me. He's talking, but I'm so adrenalised that at first I can't hear his words over the roaring in my ears. He seems earnest and impossibly young, barely out of college. I realise that he's asking what I have decided: if I'm going to accept the plea deal and life in a penal colony, or risk the death penalty if I'm found guilty.

If I'm found guilty? He's clearly as naive as he looks.

I'm about to answer when a familiar voice shouts my name. Zack is at the other end of the hallway, also cuffed and in the company of a prison escort. 'What are you gonna do?' he calls.

I try to speak but I can't find my voice. All I manage is a shrug. He disappears into the courtroom.

The prosecution team arrive. Six of them hurry behind the female exec, who strides down the hall, her stilettos ringing out on the marble floor. Her team are all dressed in similar, expensive suits and follow anxiously in her wake.

Behind them comes Detective Kitzinger, still in her battered overcoat. She walks more slowly, not part of the team. She catches my eye as she prepares to go into court and nods at me meaningfully. The message is clear – take the deal. She's almost certainly right. I can't win against the might of Sanctuary Corps.

What am I going to do?

I take my place in the dock next to Zack and Danny. Zack looks stoic, Danny gives me a nervous smile. The adjudicator is an older woman, who peers at us over her glasses. She makes us stand and asks us if we have considered the plea.

Zack and Danny take it. A life of hard labour on some godforsaken rock. It's not much of an offer – exchanging one hellish planet for another. Zack looks at me and shrugs. What else is he meant to do? I can't blame him. It's better to live, right?

An Ood stenographer sits at a small desk, typing Zack and Danny's answers onto a screen in front of it.

'And you, Ms Scott?' the judge asks. 'What have you decided?'

'I met a man,' I start clumsily. There are a few awkward chuckles in the court. I look around and realise that the public gallery is full of journalists. There are liberated Ood amongst them, working as camera operators and sound technicians. The judge raises an eyebrow.

'Whilst I was on the expedition, I mean. If you've read our statements, then you'll know who I'm talking about. His name was the Doctor. That's all I know about him, his name. I don't know where he came from or who his people were, but I did learn what kind of man he was. He valued the truth, even when it went against his own beliefs and interests. If he were here, he would tell the truth, and his story would be the same as mine. I owe my life to him, I'm not going to compromise his values just to save my skin; what would my life be worth then? I didn't kill anyone; these names you throw at me were my crewmates. My friends. A creature from before the universe killed them.'

People begin to murmur to one another. I see journalists activating their communicators.

'Those people outside believe it was the Devil. I don't know about that, but I do know it was the most destructive force I've ever encountered. I don't want your offer. I'm innocent.'

People are talking now, not bothering to keep their voices low. The adjudicator calls for order. 'You understand that there could be extreme consequences if you insist upon putting us all through a trial?'

'I do. But I stand with the Doctor.'

The adjudicator finds the paper she was looking for. 'A man who fled the scene. Who has not offered a statement. Whose actions in this Pit were not witnessed by anyone, including you, and who is the only person to face this supposed ... entity that reportedly destroyed an eighty-million-credit facility.'

'I wish I had descended with him. Who knows what we might have learnt about the universe if I had been brave enough? Some scientist I turned out to be ...'

The adjudicator cuts me off. 'Ms Scott, may I seriously suggest you consult with your legal representation before you make your decision.'

The courtroom falls silent with anticipation. The only sound comes from the stenographer, patiently typing onto its screen. I wait for the Ood to catch up with the court. It doesn't. It quietly continues to type, even though no one is speaking.

The adjudicator opens her mouth, no doubt to insist on my answer. I raise my hand to silence her and she's so surprised by my impertinence that she obeys.

'I'm sorry,' I say to the stenographer, 'I don't mean to pry, but what are you writing?'

The Ood takes a moment before realising that I am addressing it. It turns to me and blinks its large, sore-looking eyes. It holds out its communication globe, which lights up with a soft amber glow. 'What you would have learnt if you had descended into the Pit.'

'What I ... What are you talking about?'

The Ood offers its screen to me. 'That is what you asked for, isn't it? Or was I mistaken?'

I cross to its modest, plastic desk and take the screen from its outreached hand. It's covered in complex symbols, unevenly spaced vertically down the page. 'I don't recognise these words.'

The Ood cocks its head to one side, puzzled. 'That is because they are not words, they are notes.'

'Notes?'

'The Song of the Doctor.'

Something catches in my throat. 'You know the Doctor?'

'It was the Doctor who saved us. Who reconnected us to one another. We will sing his song forever.'

There's a clatter from the public gallery. An Ood camera operator has allowed its camera to fall to the ground. It begins to sing. The same simple melody that I'd heard Deedee sing in my cell. It pauses, letting the notes fade almost to nothing, before the stenographer in front of me picks up the refrain and together they turn those simple notes into a harmony. A third Ood, whose job it is to open the door for the adjudicator, joins them, and together the three of them form a chord. The chord becomes a song, and the song becomes a story.

They say music can carry you away. That songs are transportive. But nothing prepares me for what happens next. Reality flickers around me. Images flare up in front of my face: silver men stalking a city, a wolf standing on its hind legs, baying at the moon, clockwork mannequins dressed from history, lurching towards me. These images make no sense, except that at the centre of each of these scenes is a man I recognise. A man who steps between me and these nightmarish visions. A skinny man in a suit, who's willing to put himself between the darkness and the vulnerable. I watch the Doctor abseil into the Pit. I feel his hands on the metal buckles as he prepares to drop. And I am him as the last buckle unclips and we fall into the darkness.

And every single person in that courtroom falls with us.

The Doctor

That was definitely more than thirty feet. I come back to consciousness and everything hurts. Nothing seems broken, at least. My wrists and hands aren't damaged, which suggests I didn't put them out in front of me to break my fall. I must've passed out as I dropped, which again suggests it was more than thirty feet. Still, on the plus side, not a fatal fall. Not this time.

But if I landed on my face ... Oh, not the nose. I like the nose! This nose is definitely an improvement on the last one. I give it a tentative squeeze with a gloved hand. Nope, all intact. Shards of glass tinkle as they drop to the rocky floor.

My visor is broken!

In a moment of panic, I cover up the hole with my hands, but there is no need. I can breathe! There's air down here! Wherever here turns out to be. I clamber to my feet – my knees are sore. It's always the knees that go first in a body. It must be all the running up and down corridors. I should really retire the sneakers and get something with proper support for my arches. I'm not a young man.

Enough, Doctor, *focus*.

I look above me, no sign of Ida or the top of the Pit. Just blackness in every direction. So not just air to breathe, something used air to cushion my fall. Something wants me alive. Which I'm going to mark down as a plus. I love it when they don't want to kill me *straight* away.

I activate the communicator link on my wrist. 'Ida? I'm alive, have we comms?' My voice echoes – wherever I am, it makes the cavern upstairs seem like a front porch. For all I know that's what it is. 'You can breathe down here! Ida? Can you hear me? Ida?'

No Ida.

And no way to tell how long I've been out. For all I know, Ida ran out of air hours ago. Please, let the good ones live, just this once. As if in answer, I feel a gentle rumble under my feet. The rocket! A V124B Exploratory Shuttle if I'm not mistaken, and of course, I'm not; I recognise the drive signature. I'm great at recognising drive signatures. I could go on *Mastermind*; it could be my specialist subject!

I'm babbling, that's a sign of concussion, isn't it? Still, I've been concussed before. I've saved the world whilst concussed.

And while we're in the business of sending prayers, please let Rose have got away on that ship. Let her find a life, a great one, with laughter and friendship and ... oh, I should have told her. What was I so scared of? My little mayfly.

That can't be your priority now, Doctor. Focus on the task at hand. I'm missing something. What is it? Something useful, vital in fact. Light! I dig in the environmental suit's pocket and pull out a pocket torch. Let there be light and there was ...

'A cave painting!' I say out loud. 'Oh my word, so many beautiful cave paintings. I'm in a cave! Big cave! Caveman art gallery. Nice work too. All black and dark reds. On Earth they'd have done it with charcoal for the black and iron oxide for the red. This lot wouldn't have that – no wood or ochre on this planet. Off-worlders? Possibly. Probably. Hats off to the artist or artists though. It's nice work. Some kind of war scene. Stick men waging a battle against, oh hello, a giant, red, horned beast ...'

Pleased to meet you, I think I can guess your name.

'Dunno if you're getting this, Ida. Hope so, Al Bowlly said I had a lovely voice. And he ought to know. Nice man. Died in the Blitz, killed by a flying door.'

What will they say about my death, I wonder? Death by Pit? Died whilst abseiling? Not the noblest of epitaphs. Curiosity killed the Doctor? Now that's more like it. Very me. The torchlight picks out more paintings. New scenes. It looks like the stick men defeated the Beast and imprisoned it with ... vases. Interesting. Amphorae to be strictly accurate. Two of them, there to keep the creature in the Pit.

Imprisoned by ceramics, that's a new one on me. Something glints in the torchlight, at the very edge of my vision. The vases! In real life! Standing on plinths, like I'm at back at the Palace at Knossos. The drawings on the wall are accurate: the vases are amphorae. Tall, with two handles and a narrow neck. Same pattern repeats in civilisations throughout the galaxy. There's still no better way to store oil. Or wine for the matter. Minos kept a great wine cellar. Terrible father, but you couldn't knock him as a host.

I touch the nearest amphora and it gently lights up with a warm amber glow. The second, only a few feet away, follows suit. They each let out a gentle chime, making a perfect harmonic fifth between them.

Twinkle, twinkle, little star...

Maybe they're the key or the gate or the bars of a cell or ...

Something growls behind me. I freeze. The sound is so low that it makes my body physically vibrate. The hairs on the back of my neck are suddenly standing on end. I experience a physical state that is so rare for me that I don't immediately recognise it.

Fight or Flight.

I've been locked in rooms with Daleks, fixed to bombs by Cybermen, stalked by murderous mannequins, but I have never felt the urge to run as intensely as I do right now. I turn around slowly and the light from the amphorae reflects off the largest, reddest pair of trapezii I've ever seen. They're so gigantic, like two rust-belt mountains, that it takes me a moment to realise they're the muscles that allow shoulders to shrug and a head to move. I'm wondering where the head is, when it starts to appear.

I'm looking at a giant. A red giant. A giant that is hanging from chains, head bent down. A giant that is now using those enormous trapezii to lift its head and look at me. And what a head it is. A red skull, the size of a house, with twin bonfires for eyes and – what else but – huge curled horns.

I'm having an audience with the Devil.

And as if its existence is not frightening enough, if its very presence is not enough to strike terror into my core, it lunges for me, straining at the chains that bind its huge muscles, and roars in my face. Its breath is hot and sour and almost knocks me off my feet. I stagger back and take in the literal enormity of what I am in the presence of.

I sense it. Know it. This is the most evil thing in creation.

Its roar subsides and I do my best not to look intimidated. I'm not sure I succeed. It's hard to pull off not looking intimidated when you're shaking.

'I accept that you exist,' I say in my most confident tone. 'I don't have to accept what you are, but your physical existence, I give you that.'

It growls deep in its throat, a low rumble that causes a few rocks to skitter across the ground.

'But I don't understand. I was expected down here. I've been given a safe landing, and air. You need me for something. What?'

The creature doesn't answer. I won't call it the Devil, it'll have to convince me of that, and so far it's only roared at me. Which is odd, because I'm standing on a ledge, overlooking its prison. This is somewhere that's clearly been built to allow you to speak to the creature face to face. Eye to eye. Man to beast. But all it does is glower at me. I'm under no illusion that it wouldn't kill me in a second if it were free, but surely it brought me here for a reason?

'I don't understand,' I call out to it. 'Why don't you speak to me? Have I got to ... I don't know, beg an audience, or ... Is there a ritual? Some sort of incantation or summons or spell? All those things I don't believe in, are they real? Speak to me! Tell me!'

It opens its huge jaws for a moment, I think it might say something, but it only salivates, long strands of goo dribbling down onto the ground far below us.

I can feel my hair trying to curl – which it can't do in this body, but that never stops it from trying. It means either it's going to rain or ... I'm having the beginnings of an idea.

'You won't talk or ...' I *am* having an idea. It's a big one. I can feel it. 'Perhaps, just perhaps, you *can't* talk ...'

Oh yes, here it comes.

'Hold on, hold on, wait a minute, just let me ... oh!'

Here it is!

'No!'

Can it be?

'Maybe.'

It is.

'No!'

But then what else would explain it?

'Yes!'

Does it explain it?

'No!'

I slap myself on the forehead, and then instantly regret it, as my head is still sore from the fall.

'Think it through, Doctor!'

I turn to the creature. 'You spoke before, I heard your voice, an intelligent voice, more than that, brilliant! But looking at you now, all I can see is . . .'

The fire in its eyes, burning animal hatred, but just that. No intellect, no ambition, no cunning plan.

'All I can see is the Beast. The animal. Just . . . the body, you're just the body, the physical form. What happened to your mind? Where's it gone? Where's that intelligence . . . ?'

I feel a chill, deep in my hearts. 'Oh, no . . .'

I run back to the cave paintings, searching for some evidence that I'm on the right track. The Beast roars mindlessly at me.

'Hush now, Daddy's thinking. You're imprisoned, long time ago – before the universe.' I can't help but grimace at the notion. 'Before, after, sideways, in-between, doesn't matter just now.' I look at the drawing of the two jars, the horned beast below and the Black Hole above. 'It's a prison, and the prison's perfect – absolute, eternal.'

The truth smacks me in the face.

'Oh yes! Open the prison and the gravity field collapses, this planet falls into the Black Hole. If you escape, you die. Brilliant! Except! That's just the body, the body's trapped, that's all.'

Another drawing, one I hadn't noticed before: the creature, a wisp of smoke curling from its head, into one of the stick men.

'The Devil's an idea, in all those civilisations, just an idea. But an idea's hard to kill. An idea can escape! The mind, the mind of the great Beast, the mind can escape!'

It was never down here. Or at least, it escaped long before Rose and I arrived at the base. In their naivety, the crew came crashing down onto the planet and it saw its chance – its escape route! A human mind, ambitious, foolish, headstrong, and – like most human minds – with plenty of space for a stowaway. Toby. Tobias Zed. We thought it had left your body, but if it's not here, then ... Oh Ida, we came all the way down to the fiery depths of Hell, not realising its only occupant was strolling about upstairs!

'That's it!' I turn to the Beast, seeing the whole picture now. '*You* didn't give me air. Your gaolers did! They set this up, all those years ago. They need me alive! Cos if you're escaping, then ...' I smile to myself, feeling the old confidence returning. 'I've got to stop you.'

The red giant pulls at its chains and roars in my face, but now the storm of its breath is exhilarating. Does it know on some deep subconscious level that I am coming for it? I run back to the amphorae, close my hands around one of them. It looks fragile. If I hurl it to the ground, would that be enough to destroy this place?

'If I open your prison, your body is sucked into the Black Hole. The mind with it?' But then I see the truth. 'You've set a trap. Wheels within wheels. Because if I destroy this planet, then I destroy the gravity field ...'

I let go of the jar, leaving it intact. The adrenalin turns to bile in my stomach.

'The rocket. The rocket loses protection. It'll fall into the Black Hole too. I'll have to sacrifice Rose.'

The creature leans down until its face fills my vision, its eyes the size of bonfires. It opens its mouth and howls. Is that laughter? Is there some vestigial part of it still connected to its mind? I slump back on the rocky floor.

'So that's the trap. Or the test. Or the final judgement. If I kill you, I kill her . . .'

I think of Rose on that rocket. Missing me. Mourning me? But she wouldn't forever. She'd make a life out there, helping shape humanity's future. Visiting new worlds, meeting new races. She'd be able to look after herself. What am I thinking? Put that girl anywhere and she'd be nothing short of magnificent. She's the one who stopped the Nestene Consciousness when it had me beat. She's the one who found humanity in a Dalek, when I was blinded by hatred and revenge.

I turn to face the creature – whatever or whoever it is. 'I think it's fair to say that you're a schemer, and as schemes go, it's a good one. Except . . .' I can't help laughing now. 'It implies, in your big, grand scheme of gods and devils, that Rose Tyler is a victim. And, you see, I know Rose Tyler, better than anyone, better than her boyfriend, better than her mother. You could say *she's* my specialist subject.'

I go to knock the amphora off its plinth, but no,

this requires a bigger moment. It requires a bit of flair, a bit of drama. I pick up a large rock and weigh it in my hand.

'I've seen a lot of the universe. I've seen fake gods and bad gods and demi-gods and would-be-gods, and out of all of that, out of that whole pantheon, if I believe in one thing, just one thing ...' I look the Beast right in the eye. 'I believe in her.'

I heave the rock down and smash the jar.

The whole chamber begins to shudder. Flames ignite beneath the Beast. I am bringing down the temple!

'This is your freedom!' I yell at the Devil, as it starts to burn. 'Free to die! You're going into the Black Hole, and I'm riding with you!'

And with that, I hurl the rock at the second vase and it smashes into a million little pieces. The Beast howls in agony.

'Howzat!' I scream. A Time Lord victorious as a world burns!

I stumble away from the Beast, an inferno erupting from within it. Its scarlet skin bubbles black, its horns turn to ash. Debris falls from the ceiling, and I take cover below an outcropping. I want to savour my last moments. If this is how it truly ends, I don't want to miss a second of it.

Be brilliant, Rose Tyler.

And know that I love you. With both my hearts. You'll never hear these words, but that doesn't make them any less true. Now save them all. And save yourself.

Ida

The Ood hold the final note of their song and then gently bring it to a close. There's silence in the courtroom. And then, the sound of crying. Next to me, Danny wipes his eyes. I slip my arm round him and Zack does the same.

The three of us sit there, holding one another as we await confirmation of our fate. Someone else begins to sob. I look around: one of the prosecution team, a young man, cropped hair, expensive suit and a thick steel watch, is crying uncontrollably. The Song of the Doctor has got under his skin and he has no defence against the feelings erupting within him. His tears set off more; two of the journalists pull tissues from their pockets. Several people go so far as to kneel and pray. We have all been the Doctor. We have all faced the Devil. We have all known what it is to sacrifice ourselves for someone else. For everyone else.

An avalanche of emotion fills the room.

The suited exec remains unaffected by what has happened. She's staring at her sobbing underling, bemused. She grabs him angrily by the shoulders, shaking him and telling him to pull himself together. It seems not everyone can hear the Ood's song.

But you can. I see you leaning on the prosecution bench, your head hung down. Your heavy overcoat can't hide how your body trembles. When you lift your head and see me staring, you break ranks and come over to the defence table.

'It was all true?' You ask.

I nod.

'Did you know what he did down there?'

I shake my head, struggling to keep control of my own emotions. 'But it doesn't surprise me.'

I take hold of your arm, more to keep you upright than as a gesture of solidarity.

'Who was he?' You whisper.

Zack

When Ida gave her response to the plea, when she said that she wouldn't deny the existence of the

Doctor, even if it might put her life at risk, I didn't get it.

Now I do.

You see, I never let the Doctor in. I got that he was clever, special even, but I didn't appreciate how remarkable he was. How many people would choose the right action, even at the cost of their own life? The religions of the universe tend to have one thing in common. The notion that grace is restored through sacrifice. Perhaps it can *only* be restored through sacrifice.

'What happened?' I turn to see that the adjudicator is staring at us, her face flushed and tear-streaked. 'Tell us what happened next. Was the Doctor's faith in Rose justified?'

Hesitantly, not sure what this means for my plea – not sure what it means for anything – I stand on shaking legs and speak.

Every alarm on the rocket went off at the same time. Stress fractures threatened the integrity of the hull. Despite the drive operating at maximum capacity, we were losing speed.

Rose turned from the porthole and articulated my worst fears: 'It's the planet, the planet's moving, it's falling.'

And we were falling with it.

Toby yelled something I couldn't make out. He kicked the back of my chair.

I turned to face him. 'You're not helping ...'

The words died. He was having some kind of fit; horrible shudders wracked his whole body and spittle foamed at the corner of his mouth. His eyes were wide and unseeing. His safety harness dug into his throat where he strained against it. He looked like he was going to suffocate himself.

'Rose! Help him!'

She was already reaching across to his seat. I turned back to the controls for a moment. I started a diagnostic, but what was it going to tell us, other than we were about to be crushed to death, and there was nothing anyone or anything could do about it?

Toby screamed once and stopped kicking against the back of my seat.

'It's him!' Rose yelled. 'It's Toby! Zack, it's him! It's inside him! Do something! Just do something!'

'I'm trying to ...' And then I saw why she was yelling.

Toby's eyes were lit up with scarlet fire. His face was burnt with black lettering. I recognised the symbols; we'd found them on the planet. Toby told us he couldn't translate them. Well, it seemed he knew what they meant now.

'I am the Rage!' Toby screamed, his voice bitter and angry. 'I am the Bile! And the Ferocity! I am the Prince and the Fool and the Agony! I am the Sin and the Fear and the Darkness!'

I tried to speak but my mouth fell slackly open. We thought we had left the Devil in the Pit, but we had brought it with us. And unless we could do something, we would release it into the universe.

But what could we do? Danny was pushing himself against his seat, doing anything to stay as far away from Toby as possible. His face was screwed up in terror. No help there.

Toby exhaled at me and his breath ignited! I felt the heat scorch my face. I smelt my eyebrows singe.

'I shall never die!' he yelled, fixing me with his burning eyes. 'The thought of me is forever! In the bleeding hearts of men, in their vanity and obsession and lust! Nothing shall ever destroy me! Nothing!'

Another alarm joined the chorus. We'd passed the event horizon. From that moment, there could be no escaping the Black Hole. We were going to be sucked down into it, asphyxiated when it crushed the hull of the ship.

Unless the Devil got us first.

Rose was looking at me. Her face set. Scared, but determined. She turned to Toby and lifted her arm and I saw she had the bolt gun in her hand. For a moment, I thought she was going to shoot him. But then she pointed the gun past him, aiming at the cockpit window.

'Go to hell!'

She fired and the window blew out.

We lost pressure instantly. I felt as if I were caught in a sudden storm. The vacuum outside swept the air out of the cabin. Suddenly, I couldn't take a breath, I felt the icy chill of the void. What had she done?

Her hair whipping wildly around her face, Rose fought against the wind. She leaned across and with a quick fumble released Toby's safety harness. The Devil opened its mouth – to scream? To curse her? – but was sucked out of the forward window before it could form a word.

I watched with macabre fascination as Toby twisted and tumbled away from us, towards the Black Hole. His face was twisted with outrage. He was still writhing when I lost sight of him, and he became another piece of debris making its final trip across the night.

The emergency shields slid into place, sealing the cockpit. The gale dropped and I was left with ringing in my ears and the sound of oxygen being pumped into the cabin.

'You did it,' Danny whispered, staring in awe at Rose.

But facts were facts. 'We've still lost the gravitational funnel,' I said. 'We can't escape the Black Hole any more than that thing could.'

As if to prove the point, we heard an ominous creak of metal, as the hull began to stretch beyond its endurance.

'But we stopped him,' Rose said, quietly. 'That's what the Doctor would have done.'

'Yeah,' I shrugged. 'Some victory.' The ship began to shudder beneath us. 'We're going in . . .'

The rocket was dragged into a death spiral as the Black Hole exerted its grip. I brought up a graphic representation of the Black Hole on the main screen, just as the planet neared the event horizon. It appeared to slow and then froze. The time dilation caused its final moments to stretch into a ribbon, which glowed crimson, as the colour wavelengths were distorted by gravity. Finally, the planet broke up, streams of debris spiralling as they fell into the Hungry God. I didn't think it would be spitting out the Bitter Pill a second time.

Oh, Ida...

'The planet's gone,' Danny whispered. He turned to Rose. 'I'm sorry.'

'I did my best,' I said, looking over to Rose. She looked so sad, clearly thinking not of herself, but of her friend. 'But hey. We're the first human beings to fall inside a black hole, how about that? We get to make history...'

As the alarms wailed around me, and the ship groaned its last, I mouthed a silent prayer to the gods of my childhood. Then I closed my eyes and waited for the end.

It didn't come.

Emergency alarms silenced themselves one by one. Hull integrity, drive overload, life support. Angry red lights flickered and returned to green, as the rocket insisted – against all the laws of physics – that normality had been restored.

What the hell?

'What happened?' Rose asked.

'Are we dead?' Danny stammered. 'Is this the afterlife?'

If it was, I'd have gratefully embraced it, but no, according to every instrument in front of me, we were very much alive. Alive and ... manoeuvring?

'We're turning. We're turning around. We're turning away!'

There was a crackle over the comms and then a warm hum filled the cockpit. 'Sorry about the hijack, Captain,' a familiar voice said cheerily. 'This is the good ship TARDIS. Now, first things first, have you got a Rose Tyler on board?'

Behind me, Rose screamed with joy. 'I'm here! It's me! Oh my god! Where are you?'

I turned round to see her biting her fingers with excitement. She beat a rhythm on the floor with her feet and screamed again.

'But how?' I managed.

'I'm towing you home. Gravity, shmavity, my people practically invented black holes. In fact, they did. Couple of minutes, we'll be nice and safe. Oh, and Captain? Can we do a swap? Say, if you give me Rose Tyler, I'll give you Ida Scott, how about that?'

'She's alive?'

Danny was grinning with joy. I gripped his shoulder. Was this really happening?

'Bit of oxygen starvation, but she should be fine.' The Doctor paused and became more solemn. 'I couldn't save the Ood. Only had time for one trip. They went down with the planet.' There was a pause, heavy and strained. Then he brightened. 'Entering clear space. End of the line. Mission closed.'

Danny

I led Rose down to the cargo bay of the rocket. I say I led her. The truth was I could barely keep up. She practically danced her way there, laughing the whole way. The cargo bay was the largest room on the ship. A huge metal chamber, which had once contained all the interlocking segments that made up Sanctuary Base 6. It was empty now, save for the huge netting, which hung down from the ceiling, and had once been used to keep the pieces of the base secure.

Rose ran into the middle of the bay. 'Come on, then!' Her words echoed round the empty chamber. And then it began, that sound like an animal's death throes. But this time I wasn't hearing it over the tinny speakers of the security monitors. Wind appeared from nowhere, sending the netting swinging wildly above us. In the centre of the room, a light, from nowhere, white and pure, began to pulse. Beneath it, a tall, navy-blue box broke all the rules of physics.

I'd never seen Rose grin so broadly. 'I didn't think I'd ever see him again. I can't believe I got this lucky.'

'He's the lucky one.' It was the most honest thing I'd ever said to her. 'Don't let him forget it.'

Rose looked at me in puzzlement for a moment, then she understood. She gave me a big hug, told me to be good to myself, and then she ran into the blue box.

I was left staring at its closed door. There was a little sign on it, which read:

> Free For Use of Public
> Advice & Assistance
> Obtainable Immediately

Was this what they did? Spent their days flying around the galaxy in a blue box helping people and asking for nothing in return?

The noise started up again. This time it sounded like engines, ancient and protesting.

'Wait a minute!' I shouted as the box started to fade. 'What about Ida?'

But as the box disappeared, it left Ida behind, lying in the recovery position on the floor. She looked a little pale but was breathing steadily.

Zack helped me carry her to an acceleration couch in the cockpit. As we laid her down, she started to stir. Zack refused to believe that the Doctor and Rose had taken off in a box the size of a large wardrobe.

'You're saying it was like a life capsule?'

'I'm saying it was a box.'

'How can a box make the jump to hyperspace?'

'I don't know, I didn't go inside. Ask Ida!'

Zack turned to her, incredulous. 'So? What was it?'

She tried to talk but broke out into a fit of coughing. 'I don't know,' she managed croakily. 'I can't remember.'

The comms chirruped with an incoming call. On the view screen, the Doctor's blue box was orbiting us, spinning slowly as it did. Zack stared at it, speechless.

'Zack, we'll be off now. Have a good trip home. And the next time you get curious about something ... Oh, what's the point? You'll just go blundering in. The human race!'

Ida sat up. 'But Doctor ... What did you find down there? That creature, what was it?'

There was a pause, where all we could hear was the gentle hum of the Doctor's ship. 'I don't know,' he said finally. 'Never did decipher the writing. But that's good! Day I know everything, I might as well stop.'

Rose's voice came over the comms. 'But what do you think it was? Really?'

'I think we beat it. That's good enough for me.' He changed the subject. 'Right! Ida ... see you again, maybe.'

'I hope so,' she said, next to me.

'And thanks, boys!' Rose added.

Ida sat up on the couch, not ready for this conversation to end. 'Hold on though, Doctor, you never really said ... You two – who are you?'

'Oh, us? We're the stuff of legend!' he exclaimed.

And cut the connection.

Addendum

Addendum

To Tilda Crow, VP Internal Affairs

I'm writing to inform you that I no longer wish to be seconded to Sanctuary Corps. After your attempt to appeal the acquittal of Scott, Bartock and Cross Flane, I want nothing more to do with you or your organisation. I confess I was surprised by your actions. You were there, after all. You experienced what we all did in that courtroom. Not only the Doctor's bravery, but the darkness and danger that exists in the universe.

I'm returning to police work. I want to help people. To live in the light and not the shadows.

Yours,

Sandra Kitzinger, Detective, Third Class

Dear Danny,

I'm sorry I haven't written before. I meant to, particularly after I saw you on the news, being interviewed at the blockade above the Tharils' homeworld. You were brilliant, the way you and the Ood braved the laser fire from those slaver ships. My heart was in my mouth! The Friends of the Tharils are lucky to have you.

I have some news. Something I think only you and Zack could appreciate. I've tried to reach Zack at the monastery, but the Church of the Tin Vagabond don't allow their seminarians contact with the outside world, not whilst they're undergoing priestly formation. When Zack said he was joining the Church, I did wonder if he was going to join the Disciples of the Doctor. He has more right than most; at least, he's actually met the man! Apparently, of all the people in the courtroom that day, twelve of them took an oath to follow the 'example of the Doctor'. Now, every other person I meet claims they were there, claims they heard the song too. There's half a million people signed up to that cult. I wonder what the Doctor would think of that? I should have asked him when I had the chance. That's why I'm writing. I met him again. He came to see me, just like he said he might on that last day on the rocket.

He looked older, as if he'd lived through many more days than I had in the year since we'd said goodbye. Although, bizarrely, he was the wearing the same suit. Exactly the same one. Same shoes too! Nothing about that man adds up. I was at the cemetery, tidying my father's grave. I do that a lot these days. It's as good a place as any to think. I looked up and saw a blue box standing between two mausoleums. As soon as I saw it, I knew it was him. A moment later, I saw him, walking towards me, through the gravestones.

'Hello, Ida,' he said, and gave me a hug. He was always skinny, but there was something different about him. He seemed frail and I wondered if he was ill. You know, seriously ill. We sat on a bench by the grave and chatted, mostly about you and Zack. He was delighted to hear you'd become an activist, but couldn't believe Zack had found God. I asked about Rose and he said they were together and apart. When I pressed him about it, he changed the subject. He said he was doing a tour. 'Like a holiday?' I asked, but he looked away and murmured, 'No, not like that.'

I got the feeling that he wanted something from me. Absolution?

'I've been thinking a lot about our time together recently,' he said, quietly. 'About what we found in the Pit. Whether that creature really was . . .'

'The Devil?'

He nodded uncomfortably. 'I've always tried my best, Ida. But I have found myself in situations where I've had to make . . . difficult decisions.'

'You saved us all. The whole universe would have fallen if Toby had got free.'

He smiled politely, as if I were just being kind.

'I was caught up in a war on my home planet. I made a decision.' His eyes glinted with tears. 'A decision that's proved hard to live with. And now, now I'm facing . . .'

'Your death?'

He looked at me, surprised, and then nodded, almost imperceptibly. 'I can't help wondering – if there is an afterlife, a judgement day of some kind – if I'm going to be judged for those decisions.'

I took his hand in mine. It was warm, almost hot; I wondered if he had a fever. 'When the Devil spoke to us all, it said I was "still running from Daddy". It wasn't wrong.'

'You didn't get on?'

'We got on great. I was his favourite. He was a lovely bear of a man. Dementia took him early. It's one of those illnesses that, however hard they try to wipe it out, it always finds a way back. He forgot who I was at the end, who we all were. And one day, I'm visiting him in the home, and I hug him goodbye, and he tries to kiss me, you know, really kiss me. He didn't know what he was doing, or rather he didn't know who he was doing it with. But I was horrified and revolted. I couldn't bear to be near him after that, so I took a job that would take me as far away from him as possible.'

'All the way to the Bitter Pill.'

I nodded. 'He died while I was away. And now I can't put it right, because he's gone. All I can do is come here and keep the leaves off his grave. And try to do better.' I looked at the Doctor, his brown eyes looked so tired. 'It's all we can do, Doctor. Try to do better.'

We sat there in silence for a while. When he got up to go, he was unsteady on his feet. So I walked him back to his blue box, my arm linked through his. As he took the key out of his pocket, I swear his hand was faintly glowing in the evening light.

'If it *was* the Devil,' I said. 'If it's all true, Heaven and Hell and all the rest – whatever wrongs you've done in the past, I suspect you've more than made up for them.'

'I wish I could be so sure,' he said.

A few moments later, he was gone.

Lots of love,
Ida

Acknowledgements

Grateful thanks to Bethan Evans, my agent, for decades of wise words and guidance. Rebecca Levene for clear thoughts on an early draft, to Brian Hollywood and Paul Thomas for great company and encouraging words, to Steve Cole for sharp editing, and, as always, to Roderic David, for love and hugs.

Also available in the Target series from BBC Books

DOCTOR WHO
THE TIME OF ANGELS
JENNY T COLGAN

ALIENS OF LONDON

JOSEPH LIDSTER

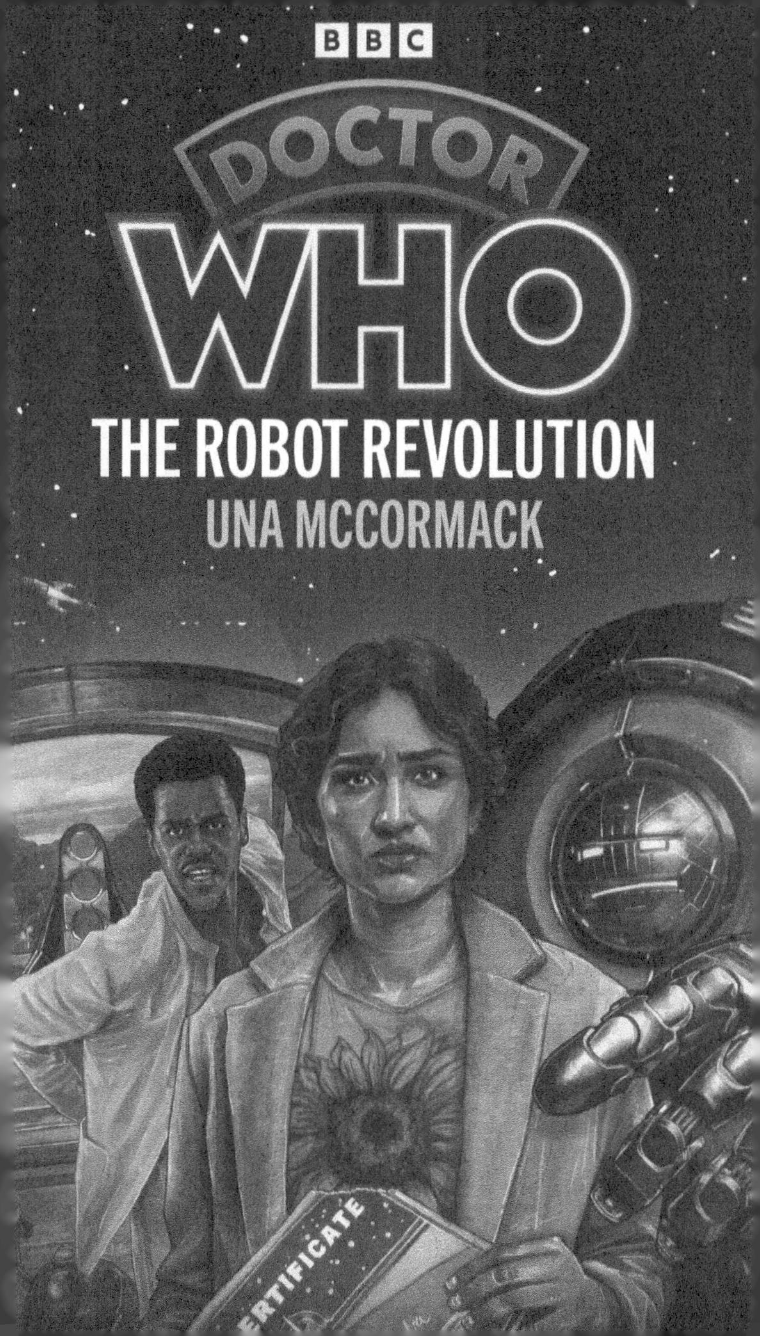

DOCTOR WHO

THE ROBOT REVOLUTION
UNA MCCORMACK